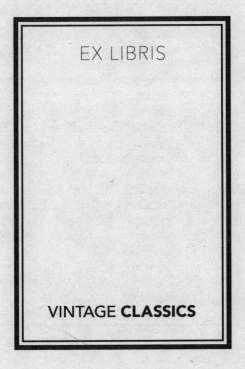

EX LIBRIS

VINTAGE **CLASSICS**

MOTHER NIGHT

Kurt Vonnegut was born in Indianapolis in 1922 and studied biochemistry at Cornell University. During the Second World War he served in Europe and, as a prisoner of war in Germany, witnessed the destruction of Dresden by Allied bombers, an experience which inspired his classic novel *Slaughterhouse-Five*. He is the author of thirteen other novels, three collections of stories and five non-fiction books.
Kurt Vonnegut died in 2007.

ALSO BY KURT VONNEGUT

KURT VONNEGUT

Mother Night

VINTAGE BOOKS
London

27 29 30 28 26

Vintage
20 Vauxhall Bridge Road,
London SW1V 2SA

Vintage Classics is part of the Penguin Random House group of companies
whose addresses can be found at global.penguinrandomhouse.com.

Copyright © Kurt Vonnegut Jr. 1961, 1966

Kurt Vonnegut has asserted his right to be identified as the author of this
Work in accordance with the Copyright, Designs and Patents Act 1988

First published in Great Britain by Jonathan Cape in 1968

www.vintage-books.co.uk

A CIP catalogue record for this book is
available from the British Library

ISBN 9780099819301

Penguin Random House is committed to a sustainable future for
our business, our readers and our planet. This book is made from
Forest Stewardship Council® certified paper.

Printed and bound in Great Britain by Clays Ltd, St Ives plc

TO MATA HARI

Breathes there the man, with soul so dead,
Who never to himself hath said,
   'This is my own, my native land!'
Whose heart hath ne'er within him burn'd
As home his footsteps he hath turn'd
   From wandering on a foreign strand?
                  —SIR WALTER SCOTT

Introduction

This is the only story of mine whose moral I know. I don't think it's a marvelous moral; I simply happen to know what it is: We are what we pretend to be, so we must be careful about what we pretend to be.

My personal experience with Nazi monkey business was limited. There were some vile and lively native American Fascists in my home town of Indianapolis during the thirties, and somebody slipped me a copy of *The Protocols of the Elders of Zion*, I remember, which was supposed to be the Jews' secret plan for taking over the world. And I remember some laughs about my aunt, too, who married a *German* German, and who had to write to Indianapolis for proofs that she had no Jewish blood. The Indianapolis mayor knew her from high school and dancing school, so he had fun putting ribbons and official seals all over the documents the Germans required, which made them look like eighteenth-century peace treaties.

After a while the war came, and I was in it, and I was captured, so I got to see a little of Germany from the inside while the war was still going on. I was a private, a battalion scout, and, under the terms of the Geneva Convention, I had to work for my keep, which was good, not bad. I didn't have to stay in prison all the time, somewhere out in the countryside. I got to go to a city, which was Dresden, and to see the people and the things they did.

There were about a hundred of us in our particular work group, and we were put out as contract labor to a factory that was making a vitamin-enriched malt syrup for pregnant women. It tasted like thin honey laced with hickory smoke. It was good. I wish I had some right now. And the city was lovely, highly ornamented, like Paris, and untouched by war. It was supposedly an 'open' city, not to be attacked since there were no troop concentrations or war industries there.

But high explosives were dropped on Dresden by American

and British planes on the night of February 13, 1945, just about twenty-one years ago, as I now write. There were no particular targets for the bombs. The hope was that they would create a lot of kindling and drive firemen underground.

And then hundreds of thousands of tiny incendiaries were scattered over the kindling, like seeds on freshly turned loam. More bombs were dropped to keep firemen in their holes, and all the little fires grew, joined one another, became one apocalyptic flame. Hey presto: fire storm. It was the largest massacre in European history, by the way. And so what?

We didn't get to see the fire storm. We were in a cool meat-locker under a slaughterhouse with our six guards and ranks and ranks of dressed cadavers of cattle, pigs, horses, and sheep. We heard the bombs walking around up there. Now and then there would be a gentle shower of calcimine. If we had gone above to take a look, we would have been turned into artifacts characteristic of fire atoms: seeming pieces of charred firewood two or three feet long – ridiculously small human beings, or jumbo fried grasshoppers, if you will.

The malt syrup factory was gone. Everything was gone but the cellars where 135,000 Hansels and Gretels had been baked like gingerbread men. So we were put to work as corpse miners, breaking into shelters, bringing bodies out. And I got to see many German types of all ages as death had found them, usually with valuables in their laps. Sometimes relatives would come to watch us dig. They were interesting, too.

So much for Nazis and me.

If I'd been born in Germany, I suppose I would have been a Nazi, bopping Jews and gypsies and Poles around, leaving boots sticking out of snowbanks, warming myself with my secretly virtuous insides. So it goes.

There's another clear moral to this tale, now that I think about it: When you're dead you're dead.

And yet another moral occurs to me now: Make love when you can. It's good for you.

Iowa City, 1966

Editor's Note

In preparing this edition of the confessions of Howard W. Campbell, Jr., I have had to deal with writings concerned with more than mere informing or deceiving, as the case may be. Campbell was a writer as well as a person accused of extremely serious crimes, a one-time playwright of moderate reputation. To say that he was a writer is to say that the demands of art alone were enough to make him lie, and to lie without seeing any harm in it. To say that he was a playwright is to offer an even harsher warning to the reader, for no one is a better liar than a man who has warped lives and passions onto something as grotesquely artificial as a stage.

And, now that I've said that about lying, I will risk the opinion that lies told for the sake of artistic effect – in the theater, for instance, and in Campbell's confessions, perhaps – can be, in a higher sense, the most beguiling forms of truth.

I don't care to argue the point. My duties as an editor are in no sense polemic. They are simply to pass on, in the most satisfactory style, the confessions of Campbell.

As for my own tinkerings with the text, they are few. I have corrected some spelling, removed some exclamation points, and all the italics are mine.

I have in several instances changed names, in order to spare embarrassment or worse to innocent persons still living. The names Bernard B. O'Hare, Harold J. Sparrow, and Dr. Abraham Epstein, for instance, are fictitious, insofar as this account goes. Also fictitious are Sparrow's Army serial number and the title I have given to an American Legion post in the text; there is no Francis X. Donovan Post of the American Legion in Brookline.

There is one point at which my accuracy rather than the accuracy of Howard W. Campbell, Jr., can be questioned. That point is in Chapter Twenty-two, in which Campbell quotes three of his poems in both English and German. In his manuscript, the English versions are perfectly clear. The German versions, however, recalled from memory by Campbell, are so hacked up and smeary with revisions as to be illegible, as often as not. Campbell was proud of himself as a writer in German, indifferent to his skill in English. In trying to justify his pride in his German, he worked over the German versions of the poems again and again and again, and was apparently never satisfied with them.

So, in order to offer some idea in this edition as to what the poems were like in German, I have had to commission a delicate job of restoration. The person who did this job, who made vases out of shards, so to speak, was Mrs. Theodore Rowley, of Cotuit, Massachusetts, a fine linguist, and a respectable poetess in her own right.

I have made significant cuts in only two places. In Chapter Thirty-nine, I have made a cut that was insisted upon by my publisher's lawyer. In the original of that chapter, Campbell has one of the Iron Guardsmen of the White Sons of the American Constitution shouting at a G-man, 'I'm a better American than you are! My father invented "I-Am-An-American Day"!' Witnesses agree that such a claim was made, but made without any apparent basis in fact. The lawyer's feeling is that to reproduce the claim in the body of the text would be to slander those persons who really did invent 'I-Am-An-American Day.'

In the same chapter, incidentally, Campbell is, according to witnesses, at his most accurate in reporting exactly what was said. The actual death speech of Resi Noth, all agree, is reproduced by Campbell, word for word.

The only other cutting I have done is in Chapter Twenty-three, which is pornographic in the original. I would have considered myself honor-bound to present that chapter unbowdlerized, were it not for Campbell's request, right in the body of the text, that some editor perform the emasculation.

The title of the book is Campbell's. It is taken from a speech by Mephistopheles in Goethe's *Faust*. As translated by Carlyle F. MacIntyre (New Directions, 1941), the speech is this:

I am a part of the part that at first was all, part of the
darkness that gave birth to light, that supercilious light
which now disputes with Mother Night her ancient rank
and space, and yet can not succeed; no matter how it
struggles, it sticks to matter and can't get free. Light
flows from substance, makes it beautiful; solids can check
its path, so I hope it won't be long till light and the
world's stuff are destroyed together.

The dedication of the book is Campbell's too. Of the dedication, Campbell wrote this in a chapter he later discarded:

Before seeing what sort of a book I was going to have
here, I wrote the dedication – 'To Mata Hari.' She
whored in the interest of espionage, and so did I.

Now that I've seen some of the book, I would prefer
to dedicate it to someone less exotic, less fantastic, more
contemporary – less of a creature of silent film.

I would prefer to dedicate it to one familiar person,
male or female, widely known to have done evil while
saying to himself, 'A very good me, the real me, a me
made in heaven, is hidden deep inside.'

I can think of many examples, could rattle them off
after the fashion of a Gilbert and Sullivan patter song.
But there is no single name to which I might aptly dedicate this book – unless it would be my own.

Let me honor myself in that fashion, then:

This book is rededicated to Howard W. Campbell, Jr.,
a man who served evil too openly and good too secretly,
the crime of his times.

KURT VONNEGUT, JR.

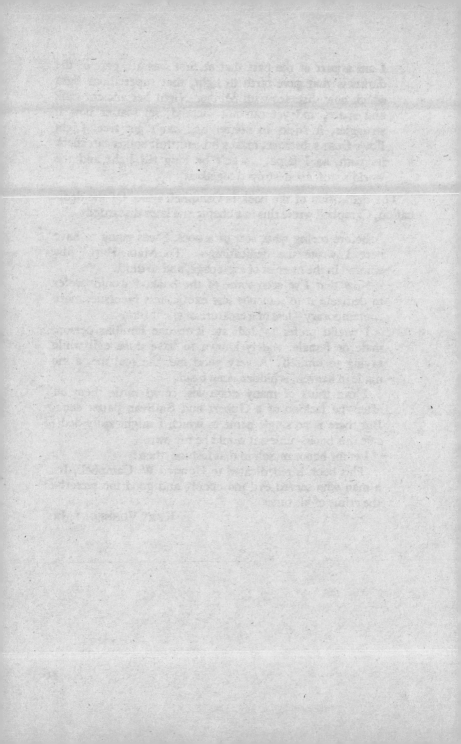

**The Confessions
of Howard W. Campbell, Jr.**

1 : Tiglath-pileser the Third . . .

My name is Howard W. Campbell, Jr.

I am an American by birth, a Nazi by reputation, and a nationless person by inclination.

The year in which I write this book is 1961.

I address this book of mine to Mr. Tuvia Friedmann, Director of the Haifa Institute for the Documentation of War Criminals, and to whomever else this may concern.

Why should this book interest Mr. Friedmann?

Because it is written by a man suspected of being a war criminal. Mr. Friedmann is a specialist in such persons. He had expressed an eagerness to have any writings I might care to add to his archives of Nazi villainy. He is so eager as to give me a typewriter, free stenographic service, and the use of research assistants, who will run down any facts I may need in order to make my account complete and accurate.

I am behind bars in a nice new jail in old Jerusalem.

I am awaiting a fair trial for my war crimes by the Republic of Israel.

It is a curious typewriter Mr. Friedmann has given to me – and an appropriate typewriter, too. It is a typewriter that was obviously made in Germany during the Second World War. How can I tell? Quite simply, for it puts at finger tips a symbol that was never used on a typewriter before the Third German Reich, a symbol that will never be used on a typewriter again.

The symbol is the twin lightning strokes used for the dreaded *S.S.*, the *Schutzstaffel*, the most fanatical wing of Nazism.

I used such a typewriter in Germany all through the war. Whenever I had occasion to write of the Schutzstaffel, which I did often and with enthusiasm, I never abbreviated it as 'S.S.,' but always struck the typewriter key for the far more frightening and magical twin lightning strokes.

Ancient history.

I am surrounded by ancient history. Though the jail in which I rot is new, some of the stones in it, I'm told, were cut in the time of King Solomon.

And sometimes, when I look out through my cell window at the gay and brassy youth of the infant Republic of Israel, I feel that I and my war crimes are as ancient as Solomon's old gray stones.

How long ago that war, that Second World War, was! How long ago the crimes in it!

How nearly forgotten it is, even by the Jews – the young Jews, that is.

One of the Jews who guards me here knows nothing about that war. He is not interested. His name is Arnold Marx. He has very red hair. He is only eighteen, which means Arnold was three when Hitler died, and nonexistent when my career as a war criminal began.

He guards me from six in the morning until noon.

Arnold was born in Israel. He has never been outside of Israel.

His mother and father left Germany in the early thirties. His grandfather, he told me, won an Iron Cross in the First World War.

Arnold is studying to be a lawyer. The avocation of Arnold and of his father, a gunsmith, is archaeology. Father and son spend most all their spare time excavating the ruins of Hazor. They do so under the direction of Yigael Yadin, who was Chief of Staff of the Israeli Army during the war with the Arab States.

So be it.

Hazor, Arnold tells me, was a Canaanite city in northern Palestine that existed at least nineteen hundred years before Christ. About fourteen hundred years before Christ, Arnold tells me, an Israelite army captured Hazor, killed all forty thousand inhabitants, and burned it down.

'Solomon rebuilt the city,' said Arnold, 'but in 732 B.C. Tiglath-pileser the Third burned it down again.'

4

'Who?' I said.

'Tiglath-pileser the Third,' said Arnold. 'The Assyrian,' he said, giving my memory a nudge.

'Oh,' I said. '*That* Tiglath-Pileser.'

'You act as though you never heard of him,' said Arnold.

'I never have,' I said. I shrugged humbly. 'I guess that's pretty terrible.'

'Well –' said Arnold, giving me a schoolmaster's frown, 'it seems to me he really *is* somebody everybody ought to know about. He was probably the most remarkable man the Assyrians ever produced.'

'Oh,' I said.

'I'll bring you a book about him, if you like,' said Arnold.

'That's nice of you,' I said. 'Maybe I'll get around to thinking about remarkable Assyrians later on. Right now my mind is pretty well occupied with remarkable Germans.'

'Like who?' he said.

'Oh, I've been thinking a lot lately about my old boss, Paul Joseph Goebbels,' I said.

Arnold looked at me blankly. 'Who?' he said.

And I felt the dust of the Holy Land creeping in to bury me, sensed how thick a dust-and-rubble blanket I would one day wear. I felt thirty or forty feet of ruined cities above me; beneath me some primitive kitchen middens, a temple or two – and then –

Tiglath-pileser the Third.

The guard who relieves Arnold Marx at noon each day is a man nearly my own age, which is forty-eight. He remembers the war, all right, though he doesn't like to.

His name is Andor Gutman. Andor is a sleepy, not very bright Estonian Jew. He spent two years in the extermination camp at Auschwitz. According to his own reluctant account, he came this close to going up a smokestack of a crematorium there:

'I had just been assigned to the *Sonderkommando*,' he said to me, 'when the order came from Himmler to close the ovens down.'

Sonderkommando means special detail. At Auschwitz it meant a very special detail indeed – one composed of prisoners whose duties were to shepherd condemned persons into gas chambers, and then to lug their bodies out. When the job was done, the members of the Sonderkommando were themselves killed. The first duty of their successors was to dispose of their remains.

Gutman told me that many men actually volunteered for the Sonderkommando.

'Why?' I asked him.

'If you would write a book about that,' he said, 'and give the answer to that question, that "Why?" – you would have a very great book.'

'Do you know the answer?' I said.

'No,' he said. 'That is why I would pay a great deal of money for a book with the answer in it.'

'Any guesses?' I said.

'No,' he said, looking me straight in the eye, 'even though I was one of the ones who volunteered.'

He went away for a little while, after having confessed that. And he thought about Auschwitz, the thing he liked least to think about. And he came back, and he said to me:

'There were loudspeakers all over the camp,' he said, 'and they were never silent for long. There was much music played through them. Those who were musical told me it was often good music – sometimes the best.'

'That's interesting,' I said.

'There was no music by Jews,' he said. 'That was forbidden.'

'Naturally,' I said.

'And the music was always stopping in the middle,' he said, 'and then there was an announcement. All day long, music and announcements.'

'Very modern,' I said.

He closed his eyes, remembered gropingly. 'There was one announcement that was always crooned, like a nursery rhyme. Many times a day it came. It was the call for the Sonderkommando.'

'Oh?' I said.

'*Leichenträger zur Wache*,' he crooned, his eyes still closed.

Translation: 'Corpse-carriers to the guardhouse.' In an institution in which the purpose was to kill human beings by the millions, it was an understandably common cry.

'After two years of hearing that call over the loudspeakers, between the music,' Gutman said to me, 'the position of corpse carrier suddenly sounded like a very good job.'

'I can understand that,' I said.

'You can?' he said. He shook his head. 'I can't,' he said. 'I will always be ashamed. Volunteering for the Sonderkommando – it was a very shameful thing to do.'

'I don't think so,' I said.

'I do,' he said. 'Shameful,' he said. 'I never want to talk about it again.'

3: Briquets...

The guard who relieves Andor Gutman at six each night is Arpad Kovacs. Arpad is a Roman candle of a man; loud and gay.

When Arpad came on duty at six last night, he demanded to see what I'd written so far. I gave him the very few pages, and Arpad walked up and down the corridor, waving and praising the pages extravagantly.

He didn't read them. He praised them for what he imagined to be in them.

'Give it to the complacent bastards!' he said last night. 'Tell those smug briquets!'

By briquets he meant people who did nothing to save their own lives or anybody else's life when the Nazis took over, who were willing to go meekly all the way to the gas chambers, if that was where the Nazis wanted them to go. A briquet, of course, is a molded block of coal dust, the soul of convenience where transportation, storage and combustion are concerned.

Arpad, faced with the problem of being a Jew in Nazi Hungary, did not become a briquet. On the contrary, Arpad got himself false papers and joined the Hungarian S.S.

That fact is the basis for his sympathy with me. 'Tell them the things a man does to stay alive! What's so noble about being a briquet?' he said last night.

'Did you ever hear any of my broadcasts?' I asked him. The medium of my war crimes was radio broadcasting. I was a Nazi radio propagandist, a shrewd and loathsome anti-Semite.

'No,' he said.

So I showed him a transcript of a broadcast, a transcript furnished to me by the Haifa Institute. 'Read it,' I said.

'I don't have to,' he said. 'Everybody was saying the same things over and over and over in those days.'

'Read it anyway – as a favor,' I said.

So he read it, his face becoming sourer and sourer. He handed it back to me. 'You disappoint me,' he said.

'Oh?' I said.

'It's so weak!' he said. 'It has no body, no paprika, no zest! I thought you were a master of racial invective!'

'I'm not?' I said.

'If any member of my S.S. platoon had spoken in such a friendly way about the Jews,' said Arpad, 'I would have had him shot for treason! Goebbels should have fired you and hired me as the radio scourge of the Jews. I would have raised blisters around the world!'

'You were already doing your part with your S.S. platoon,' I said.

Arpad beamed, remembering his S.S. days. 'What an Aryan I made!' he said.

'Nobody ever suspected you?' I said.

'How would they dare?' he said. 'I was such a pure and terrifying Aryan that they even put me in a special detachment. Its mission was to find out how the Jews always knew what the S.S. was going to do next. There was a leak somewhere, and we were out to stop it.' He looked bitter and affronted, remembering it, even though he had been that leak.

'Was the detachment successful in its mission?' I said.

'I'm happy to say,' said Arpad, 'that fourteen S.S. men were shot on our recommendation. Adolf Eichmann himself congratulated us.'

'You met him, did you?' I said.

'Yes —' said Arpad, 'and I'm sorry I didn't know at the time how important he was.'

'Why?' I said.

'I would have killed him,' said Arpad.

Bernard Mengel, a Polish Jew who guards me from midnight until six in the morning, is also a man my age. He once saved his own life in the Second World War by playing so dead that a German soldier pulled out three of his teeth without suspecting that Mengel was not a corpse.

The soldier wanted Mengel's three gold inlays.

He got them.

Mengel tells me that I sleep very noisily here in jail, tossing and talking all night.

'You are the only man I ever heard of,' Mengel said to me this morning, 'who has a bad conscience about what he did in the war. Everybody else, no matter what side he was on, no matter what he did, is sure a good man could not have acted in any other way.'

'What makes you think I have a bad conscience?' I said.

'The way you sleep – the way you dream,' he said. 'Even Hoess did not sleep like that. He slept like a saint, right up to the end.'

Mengel was speaking of Rudolf Franz Hoess, the commandant of the extermination camp at Auschwitz. In his tender care, literally millions of Jews were gassed. Mengel knew a little about Hoess. Before emigrating to Israel in 1947, Mengel helped to hang Hoess.

And he didn't do it with testimony, either. He did it with his two big hands. 'When Hoess was hanged,' he told me, 'the strap around his ankles – I put that on and made it tight.'

'Did that give you a lot of satisfaction?' I said.

'No,' he said. 'I was like almost everybody who came through that war.'

'What do you mean?' I said.

'I got so I couldn't feel anything,' said Mengel. 'Every job was a job to do, and no job was any better or any worse than any other.

10

'After we finished hanging Hoess,' Mengel said to me, 'I packed up my clothes to go home. The catch on my suitcase was broken, so I buckled it shut with a big leather strap. Twice within an hour I did the very same job – once to Hoess and once to my suitcase. Both jobs felt about the same.'

5 : 'Last Full Measure...'

I, too, knew Rudolf Hoess, Commandant of Auschwitz. I met
him at a New Year's Eve party in Warsaw during the war –
the start of 1944.

Hoess heard that I was a writer, and he got me to one side
at the party, and he said he wished he could write.

'How I envy you creative people –' he said to me. 'Creativity is a gift from the gods.'

Hoess said he had some marvelous stories to tell. He said
they were all true, but that people wouldn't be able to believe
them.

Hoess could not tell me the stories, he said, until the war
was won. After the war, he said, we might collaborate.

'I can talk it,' he said, 'but I can't write it.' He looked to me
for pity. 'When I sit down to write,' he said, 'I freeze.'

What was I doing in Warsaw?

I had been ordered there by my boss, Reichsleiter Dr. Paul
Joseph Goebbels, Head of the German Ministry of Popular
Enlightenment and Propaganda. I had a certain amount of
skill as a dramatist, and Dr. Goebbels wanted me to use it.
Dr. Goebbels wanted me to write a pageant honoring the German soldiers who had given their last full measure of devo-
tion – who had died, that is – in putting down the uprising of
the Jews in the Warsaw Ghetto.

Dr. Goebbels had a dream of producing the pageant annu-
ally in Warsaw after the war, of letting the ruins of the ghetto
stand forever as a setting for it.

'There would be Jews in the pageant?' I asked him.

'Certainly –' he said, 'thousands of them.'

'May I ask, sir,' I said, 'where you expect to find any Jews
after the war?'

He saw the humor in this. 'A very good question,' he said,
chuckling. 'We'll have to take that up with Hoess,' he said.

'With whom?' I said. I hadn't yet been to Warsaw, hadn't yet met with brother Hoess.

'He's running a little health resort for Jews in Poland,' said Goebbels. 'We must be sure to ask him to save us some.'

Can the writing of this ghastly pageant be added to the list of my war crimes? No, thank God. It never got much beyond having a working title, which was: 'Last Full Measure.'

I am willing to admit, however, that I probably would have written it if there had been enough time, if my superiors had put enough pressure on me.

Actually, I am willing to admit almost anything.

About this pageant: it had one peculiar result. It brought the Gettysburg Address of Abraham Lincoln to the attention of Goebbels, and then to the attention of Hitler himself.

Goebbels asked me where I'd gotten the working title, so I made a translation for him of the entire Gettysburg Address.

He read it, his lips moving all the time. 'You know,' he said to me, 'this is a very fine piece of propaganda. We are never as modern, as far ahead of the past as we like to think we are.'

'It's a very famous speech in my native land,' I said. 'Every schoolchild has to learn it by heart.'

'Do you miss America?' he said.

'I miss the mountains, the rivers, the broad plains, the forests,' I said. 'But I could never be happy there with the Jews in charge of everything.'

'They will be taken care of in due time,' he said.

'I live for that day – my wife and I live for that day,' I said.

'How is your wife?' he said.

'Blooming, thank you,' I said.

'A beautiful woman,' he said.

'I'll tell her you said so,' I said. 'It will please her immensely.'

'About the speech by Abraham Lincoln –' he said.

'Sir –?' I said.

'There are phrases in here that might be used most impressively in dedications of German military cemeteries,' he said. 'I haven't been happy at all, frankly, with most of our funeral oratory. This seems to have the extra dimension I've been looking for. I'd like very much to send this to Hitler.'

'Whatever you say, sir,' I said.

'Lincoln wasn't a Jew, was he?' he said.

'I'm not sure,' I said.

'It would be very embarrassing to me if he turned out to be one,' he said.

'I've never heard anyone suggest that he was,' I said.

'The name Abraham is very suspicious, to say the least,' said Goebbels.

'I'm sure his parents didn't realize that it was a Jewish name,' I said. 'They must have just liked the sound of it. They were simple frontier people. If they'd known the name was Jewish, I'm sure they would have called him something more American, like George or Stanley or Fred.'

Two weeks later, the Gettysburg Address came back from Hitler. There was a note from *der Fuehrer* himself stapled to the top of it. 'Some parts of this,' he wrote, 'almost made me weep. All northern peoples are one in their deep feelings for soldiers. It is perhaps our greatest bond.'

Strange – I never dream of Hitler or Goebbels or Hoess or Goering or any of the other nightmare people of the world war numbered 'two.' I dream of women, instead.

I asked Bernard Mengel, the guard who watches over me while I sleep here in Jerusalem, if he had any clues as to what I dreamed about.

'Last night?' he said.

'Any night,' I said.

'Last night it was women,' he said. 'Two names you said over and over.'

'What were they?' I said.

'Helga was one,' he said.

'My wife,' I said.

'The other was Resi,' he said.

'My wife's younger sister,' I said. 'Just their names – that's all.'

'You said "Goodbye," ' he said.

'Goodbye,' I echoed. That certainly made sense, whether I dreamed or not. Helga and Resi were both gone forever.

'And you talked about New York,' said Mengel. 'You mumbled, and then you said "New York," and then you mumbled some more.'

That made sense, too, as do most of the things I dream. I lived in New York for a long time before coming to Israel.

'New York City must be Heaven,' said Mengel.

'It might well be for you,' I said. 'It was hell for me – or not Hell, something worse than Hell.'

'What could be worse than Hell?' he said.

'Purgatory,' I said.

6: Purgatory...

About that purgatory of mine in New York City: I was in it for fifteen years.

I disappeared from Germany at the end of the Second World War. I reappeared, unrecognized, in Greenwich Village. There I rented a depressing attic apartment with rats squeaking and scrabbling in the walls. I continued to inhabit that attic until a month ago, when I was brought to Israel for trial.

There was one pleasant thing about my ratty attic: the back window of it overlooked a little private park, a little Eden formed by joined back yards. That park, that Eden, was walled off from the streets by houses on all sides.

It was big enough for children to play hide-and-seek in.

I often heard a cry from that little Eden, a child's cry that never failed to make me stop and listen. It was the sweetly mournful cry that meant a game of hide-and-seek was over, that those still hiding were to come out of hiding, that it was time to go home.

The cry was this: 'Olly-olly-ox-in-free.'

And I, hiding from many people who might want to hurt or kill me, often longed for someone to give that cry for me, to end my endless game of hide-and-seek with a sweet and mournful –

'Olly-olly-ox-in-free.'

16

I, Howard W. Campbell, Jr., was born in Schenectady, New York, on February 16, 1912. My father, who was raised in Tennessee, the son of a Baptist minister, was an engineer in the Service Engineering Department of the General Electric Company.

The mission of the Service Engineering Department was to install, maintain and repair General Electric heavy equipment sold anywhere in the world. My father, whose assignments were at first only in the United States, was rarely home. And his job demanded such varied forms of technical cleverness of him that he had scant time and imagination left over for anything else. The man was the job and the job was the man.

The only nontechnical book I ever saw him look at was a picture history of the First World War. It was a big book, with pictures a foot high and a foot-and-a-half wide. My father never seemed to tire. of looking at the book, though he hadn't been in the war.

He never told me what the book meant to him, and I never asked him. All he ever said to me about it was that it wasn't for children, that I wasn't to look at it.

So, of course, I looked at it every time I was left alone. There were pictures of men hung on barbed-wire, mutilated women, bodies stacked like cordwood – all the usual furniture of world wars.

My mother was the former Virginia Crocker, the daughter of a portrait photographer from Indianapolis. She was a housewife and an amateur cellist. She played cello with the Schenectady Symphony Orchestra, and she once had dreams of my playing the cello, too.

I failed as a cellist because I, like my father, am tone-deaf.

I had no brothers and sisters, and my father was seldom home. So I was for many years the principal companion of my mother. She was a beautiful, talented, morbid person. I think she was drunk most of the time. I remember a time when she filled a saucer with a mixture of rubbing alcohol and table salt. She put the saucer on the kitchen table, turned out all the lights, and had me sit facing her across the table.

And then she touched off the mixture with a match. The flame was almost pure yellow, a sodium flame, and it made her look like a corpse to me, made me look like a corpse to her.

'There –' she said, 'that's what we'll look like when we're dead.'

This queer demonstration not only scared me; it scared her, too. My mother scared herself with her own queerness, and from that moment on I ceased to be her companion. From that moment on she hardly spoke to me – cut me dead, I'm sure, out of fear of doing or saying something even crazier.

All that happened in Schenectady, before I was ten.

In 1923, when I was eleven, my father was assigned to the General Electric Office in Berlin, Germany. From then on, my education, my friends, and my principal language were German.

I eventually became a playwright in the German language, and I took a German wife, the actress Helga Noth. Helga Noth was the elder of the two daughters of Werner Noth, the Chief of Police of Berlin.

My father and mother left Germany in 1939, when war came.

My wife and I stayed on.

I earned my keep until the war ended in 1945 as a writer and broadcaster of Nazi propaganda to the English-speaking world. I was the leading expert on American problems in the Ministry of Popular Enlightenment and Propaganda.

When the war was ending, I was high on the list of war criminals, largely because my offenses were so obscenely public.

I was captured by one Lieutenant Bernard B. O'Hare of the American Third Army near Hersfeld on April 12, 1945. I was on a motorcycle, unarmed. While entitled to a uniform,

18

a blue and gold one, I was not wearing it. I was in mufti, in a blue serge suit and a moth-eaten coat with a fur collar.

As it happened, the Third Army had overrun Ohrdruf, the first Nazi death camp the Americans were to see, two days before. I was taken there, was forced to look at it all – the lime pits, the gallows, the whipping posts – at the gutted and scabby, bug-eyed, spavined dead in heaps.

The idea was to show me the consequences of what I had done.

The Ohrdruf gallows were capable of hanging six at a time. When I saw them, there was a dead camp guard at the end of each rope.

And it was expected that I would hang soon, too.

I expected it myself, and I took an interest in the peace of the six guards at the ends of their ropes.

They had died fast.

My photograph was taken while I looked up at the gallows. Lieutenant O'Hare was standing behind me, lean as a young wolf, as full of hatred as a rattlesnake.

The picture was on the cover of *Life*, and came close to winning a Pulitzer Prize.

I did not hang.

I committed high treason, crimes against humanity, and crimes against my own conscience, and I got away with them until now.

I got away with them because I was an American agent all through the war. My broadcasts carried coded information out of Germany.

The code was a matter of mannerisms, pauses, emphases, coughs, seeming stumbles in certain key sentences. Persons I never saw gave me my instructions, told me in which sentences of a broadcast the mannerisms were to appear. I do not know to this day what information went out through me. From the simplicity of most of my instructions, I gather that I was usually giving yes or no answers to questions that had been put to the spy apparatus. Occasionally, as during the build-up for the Normandy invasion, my instructions were more complicated, and my phrasing and diction sounded like the last stages of double pneumonia.

That was the extent of my usefulness to the Allied cause.

And that usefulness was what saved my neck.

I was provided with cover. I was never acknowledged as an American agent, but the treason case against me was sabotaged. I was freed on nonexistent technicalities about my citizenship, and I was helped to disappear.

I came to New York under an assumed name. I started a new life, in a manner of speaking, in my ratty attic overlooking ing the secret park.

I was left alone – so much alone that I was able to take back my own name, and almost nobody wondered if I was *the* Howard W. Campbell, Jr.

I would occasionally find my name in a newspaper or magazine – never as an important person, but as one name in a long list of names of war criminals who had disappeared. There were rumors of me in Iran, Argentina, Ireland. . . . Israeli agents were said to be looking high and low for me.

Be that as it may, no agent ever knocked on my door. Nobody knocked on my door, even though the name on my mailbox was plain for anybody to see: Howard W. Campbell, Jr.

Until the very end of my purgatory in Greenwich Village, the closest I came to being detected in my infamy was when I went to a Jewish doctor in the same building as my attic. I had an infected thumb.

The doctor's name was Abraham Epstein. He lived with his mother on the second floor. They had just moved in.

When I gave him my name, it meant nothing to him, but it did mean something to his mother. Epstein was young, fresh out of medical school. His mother was old – heavy, slow, deeply lined, sadly, bitterly watchful.

'That is a very famous name,' she said. 'You must know that.'

'Pardon me?' I said.

'You do not know about anybody else named Howard W. Campbell, Jr?' she said.

'I suppose there are some others,' I said.

'How old are you?' she said.

I told her.

'Then you are old enough to remember the war,' she said.

'Forget the war,' her son said to her, affectionately but sharply. He was bandaging my thumb.

'And you never heard Howard W. Campbell, Jr., broadcasting from Berlin?' she said to me.

'I do remember now – yes,' I said. 'I'd forgotten. That was a long time ago. I never listened to him, but I remember he was in the news. Those things fade.'

'They should fade,' said young Dr. Epstein. 'They belong to a period of insanity that should be forgotten as quickly as possible.'

'Auschwitz,' said his mother.

'Forget Auschwitz,' said Dr. Epstein.

'Do you know what Auschwitz was?' his mother asked me.

'Yes,' I said.

'That was where I spent my young womanhood,' she said. 'And that was where my son the doctor here spent his childhood.'

'I never think about it,' said Dr. Epstein abruptly. 'There – that thumb should be all right in a couple of days. Keep it warm, keep it dry.' And he hustled me toward the door.

'*Sprechen Sie deutsch?*' his mother called after me as I was leaving.

'Pardon me?' I said.

'I asked if you spoke German,' she said.

'Oh,' I said. 'No – I'm afraid not,' I said. I experimented shyly with the language. '*Nein?*' I said. 'That's no, isn't it?'

'Very good,' she said.

'*Auf wiedersehen,*' I said. 'That's goodbye, isn't it?'

'Until we meet again,' she said.

'Oh,' I said. 'Well – *auf wiedersehen.*'

'*Auf wiedersehen,*' she said.

9: Enter My Blue Fairy Godmother . . .

I was recruited as an American agent in 1938, three years before America got into the war. I was recruited one spring day in the Tiergarten in Berlin.

I had been married to Helga Noth a month.

I was twenty-six.

I was a fairly successful playwright, writing in the language in which I write best, German. I had one play, 'The Goblet,' running in both Dresden and Berlin. Another play of mine, 'The Snow Rose,' was then in production in Berlin. I had just finished a third one, 'Seventy Times Seven.' All three plays were medieval romances, about as political as chocolate *éclairs*.

I was sitting alone on a park bench in the sunshine that day, thinking of a fourth play that was beginning to write itself in my mind. It gave itself a title, which was *'Das Reich der Zwei'* – 'Nation of Two.'

It was going to be about the love my wife and I had for each other. It was going to show how a pair of lovers in a world gone mad could survive by being loyal only to a nation composed of themselves – a nation of two.

On a bench across the path from me a middle-aged American now sat down. He looked like a fool and a gasbag. He untied his shoelaces to relieve his feet, and he began to read a month-old copy of the Chicago *Sunday Tribune*.

Three handsome young officers of the S.S. stalked down the walk between us.

When they were gone, the man put his paper down and spoke to me in twanging Chicago English. 'Nice-looking men,' he said.

'I suppose,' I said.

'You understand English?' he said.

'Yes,' I said.

'Thank God for somebody who can understand English,'

he said. 'I've been going crazy trying to find somebody to talk to.'

'That so?' I said.

'What do you think of all this –' he said, 'or aren't people supposed to go around asking questions like that?'

'All what?' I said.

'The things going on in Germany,' he said. 'Hitler and the Jews and all that.'

'It isn't anything I can control,' I said, 'so I don't think about it.'

He nodded. 'None of your beeswax, eh?' he said.

'Pardon me?' I said.

'None of your business,' he said.

'That's right,' I said.

'You didn't understand that – when I said "beeswax" instead of "business"?' he said.

'It's a common expression, is it?' I said.

'In America it is,' he said. 'You mind if I come over there, so we don't have to holler?'

'As you please,' I said.

'As you please,' he echoed, coming over to my bench. 'That sounds like something an Englishman would say.'

'American,' I said.

He raised his eyebrows. 'Is that a fact? I was trying to guess what maybe you were, but I wouldn't have guessed that.'

'Thank you,' I said.

'You figure that's a compliment?' he said. 'That's why you said, "Thank you"?'

'Not a compliment – or an insult, either,' I said. 'Nationalities just don't interest me as much as they probably should.'

This seemed to puzzle him. 'Any of my beeswax what you do for a living?' he said.

'Writer,' I said.

'Is that a fact?' he said. 'That's a great coincidence. I was sitting over there wishing I could write, on account of I've thought up what I think's a pretty good spy story.'

'That so?' I said.

'I might as well give it to you,' he said. 'I'll never write it.'

'I've got all the projects I can handle now,' I said.

'Well – some time you may run dry,' he said, 'and then you can use this thing of mine. There's this young American, see, who's been in Germany so long he's practically a German himself. He writes plays in German, and he's married to a beautiful German actress, and he knows a lot of big-shot Nazis who like to hang around theater people.' He rattled off the names of Nazis, great and small – all of whom Helga and I knew pretty well.

It wasn't that Helga and I were crazy about Nazis. I can't say, on the other hand, that we hated them. They were a big enthusiastic part of our audience, important people in the society in which we lived.

They were people.

Only in retrospect can I think of them as trailing slime behind.

To be frank – I can't think of them as doing that even now. I knew them too well as people, worked too hard in my time for their trust and applause.

Too hard.

Amen.

Too hard.

'Who are you?' I said to the man in the park.

'Let me finish my story first,' he said. 'So this young man knows there's a war coming, figures America's gonna be on one side and Germany's gonna be on the other. So this American, who hasn't been anything but polite to the Nazis up to then, decided to pretend he's a Nazi himself, and he stays on in Germany when war comes along, and he gets to be a very useful American spy.'

'You know who I am?' I said.

'Sure,' he said. He took out his billfold, showed me a United States War Department identification card that said he was Major Frank Wirtanen, unit unspecified. 'And that's who I am. I'm asking you to be an American intelligence agent, Mr. Campbell.'

'Oh Christ,' I said. I said it with anger and fatalism. I slumped down. When I straightened up again, I said, 'Ridiculous. No – hell, no.'

'Well –' he said, 'I'm not too let-down, actually, because today isn't when you give me your final answer anyway.'

'If you imagine that I'm going home to think it over,' I said, 'you're mistaken. When I go home, it will be to have a fine meal with my beautiful wife, to listen to music, to make love to my wife, and to sleep like a log. I'm not a soldier, not a political man. I'm an artist. If war comes, I won't do anything to help it along. If war comes, it'll find me still working at my peaceful trade.'

He shook his head. 'I wish you all the luck in the world, Mr. Campbell,' he said, 'but this war isn't going to let anybody stay in a peaceful trade. And I'm sorry to say it,' he said, 'but the worse this Nazi thing gets, the less you're gonna sleep like a log at night.'

'We'll see,' I said tautly.

'That's right – we'll see,' he said. 'That's why I said you wouldn't give me your final answer today. You'll live your final answer. If you decide to go ahead with it, you'll go ahead with it strictly on your own, working your way up with the Nazis as high as you can go.'

'Charming,' I said.

'Well – it has this much charm to it –' he said, 'you'd be an authentic hero, about a hundred times braver than any ordinary man.'

A ramrod Wehrmacht general and a fat, briefcase-carrying German civilian passed in front of us, talking with suppressed excitement.

'Howdy do,' Major Wirtanen said to them amiably.

They snorted in contempt, walked on.

'You'll be volunteering right at the start of a war to be a dead man. Even if you live through the war without being caught, you'll find your reputation gone – and probably very little to live for,' he said.

'You make it sound very attractive,' I said.

'I think there's a chance I've made it attractive to *you*,' he said. 'I saw the play you've got running now, and I've read the one you're going to open.'

'Oh?' I said. 'And what did you learn from those?'

He smiled. 'That you admire pure hearts and heroes,' he said. 'That you love good and hate evil,' he said, 'and that you believe in romance.'

He didn't mention the best reason for expecting me to go on and be a spy. The best reason was that I was a ham. As a spy of the sort he described, I would have an opportunity for some pretty grand acting. I would fool everyone with my brilliant interpretation of a Nazi, inside and out.

And I *did* fool everybody. I began to strut like Hitler's right-hand man, and nobody saw the honest me I hid so deep inside.

Can I prove I was an American spy? My unbroken, lily-white neck is Exhibit A, and it's the only exhibit I have. Those whose duty it is to find me guilty or innocent of crimes against humanity are welcome to examine it in detail.

The Government of the United States neither confirms nor denies that I was an agent of theirs. That's a little something, anyway, that they don't deny the possibility.

They twitch away that tid-bit, however, by denying that a Frank Wirtanen ever served that Government in any branch. Nobody believes in him but me. So I will hereinafter speak of him often as 'My Blue Fairy Godmother.'

One of the many things my Blue Fairy Godmother told me was the sign and countersign that would identify me to my contact and my contact to me, if war should come.

The sign was: 'Make new friends.'

The countersign was: 'But keep the old.'

My lawyer here, the learned counsel for the defense, is a Mr. Alvin Dobrowitz. He grew up in America, something I never did, and Mr. Dobrowitz tells me that the sign and countersign are part of a song often sung by an idealistic American girls' organization called 'The Brownies.'

The full lyric, according to Mr. Dobrowitz, is:

Make new friends,
But keep the old.
One is si-il-ver,
The o-ther's gold.

My wife never knew I was a spy.

I would have lost nothing by telling her. My telling her wouldn't have made her love me less. My telling her wouldn't have put me in any danger. It would simply have made my heavenly Helga's world, which was already something to make The Book of Revelation seem pedestrian.

The war was enough without that.

My Helga believed that I meant the nutty things I said on the radio, said at parties. We were always going to parties.

We were a very popular couple, gay and patriotic. People used to tell us that we cheered them up, made them want to go on. And Helga didn't go through the war simply looking decorative, either. She entertained the troops, often within the sound of enemy guns.

Enemy guns? Somebody's guns, anyway.

That was how I lost her. She was entertaining troops in the Crimea, and the Russians took the Crimea back. My Helga was presumed dead.

After the war, I paid a good deal of my money to a private detective agency in West Berlin to trace the wispiest word of her. Results: zero. My standing offer to the agency, unclaimed, was a prize of ten thousand dollars for clear proof that my Helga was either alive or dead.

Hi ho.

My Helga believed I meant the things I said about the races of man and the machines of history – and I was grateful. No matter what I was really, no matter what I really meant, un-critical love was what I needed – and my Helga was the angel who gave it to me.

Copiously.

No young person on earth is so excellent in all respects as to need no uncritical love. Good Lord – as youngsters play their parts in political tragedies with casts of billions, uncritical love is the only real treasure they can look for.

Das Reich der Zwei, the nation of two my Helga and I had – its territory, the territory we defended so jealously, didn't go much beyond the bounds of our great double bed.

Flat, tufted, springy little country, with my Helga and me for mountains.

And, with nothing in my life making sense but love, what a student of geography I was! What a map I could draw for a tourist a micron high, a submicroscopic *Wandervögel* bicycling between a mole and a curly golden hair on either side of my Helga's belly button. If this image is in bad taste, God help me. Everybody is supposed to play games for mental health. I have simply described the game, an adult interpretation of 'This-Little-Piggy,' that was ours.

Oh, how we clung, my Helga and I – how *mindlessly* we clung!

We didn't listen to each other's words. We heard only the melodies in our voices. The things we listened for carried no more intelligence than the purrs and growls of big cats.

If we had listened for more, had thought about what we heard, what a nauseated couple we would have been! Away from the sovereign territory of our nation of two, we talked like the patriotic lunatics all around us.

But it did not count.

Only one thing counted –

The nation of two.

And when that nation ceased to be, I became what I am today and what I always will be, a stateless person.

I can't say I wasn't warned. The man who recruited me that spring day in the Tiergarten so long ago now – that man told my fortune pretty well.

'To do your job right,' my Blue Fairy Godmother told me, 'you'll have to commit high treason, have to serve the enemy well. You won't ever be forgiven for that, because there isn't any legal device by which you can be forgiven.'

30

'The most that will be done for you,' he said, 'is that your neck will be saved. But there will be no magic time when you will be cleared, when America will call you out of hiding with a cheerful: Olly-olly-ox-in-free.'

11: War Surplus...

My mother and father died. Some say they died of broken hearts. They died in their middle sixties, at any rate, when hearts break easily.

They did not live to see the end of the war, nor did they ever see their beamish boy again. They did not disinherit me, though they must have been bitterly tempted to do so. They bequeathed to Howard W. Campbell, Jr., the notorious anti-Semite, turncoat and radio star, stocks, real estate, cash and personal property which were, in 1945, at the time of probate, worth forty-eight thousand dollars.

That boodle, through growth and inflation, has come to be worth four times that much now, giving me an unearned income of seven thousand dollars a year.

Say what you like about me, I have never touched my principal.

During my postwar years as an odd duck and recluse in Greenwich Village, I lived on about four dollars a day, rent included, and I even had a television set.

My new furnishings were all war surplus, like myself – a narrow steel cot, olive-drab blankets with 'U.S.A.' on them, folding canvas chairs, mess kits to cook in and eat out of. Even my library was largely war surplus, coming as it did from recreation kits intended for troops overseas.

And, since phonograph records came in these unused kits, too, I got myself a war-surplus, weatherproofed, portable phonograph, guaranteed to play in any climate from the Bering Straits to the Arafura Sea. By buying the recreation kits, each one a sealed pig-in-a-poke, I came into possession of twenty-six recordings of Bing Crosby's 'White Christmas.'

My overcoat, my raincoat, my jacket, my socks and my underwear were war surplus, too.

By buying a war-surplus first-aid kit for a dollar, I also came into possession of a quantity of morphine. The buzzards in the war-surplus business were so glutted with carrion as to have overlooked it.

I was tempted to take the morphine, reflecting that, if it made me feel happy, I would, after all, have enough money to support the habit. But then I understood that I was already drugged.

I was feeling no pain.

My narcotic was what had got me through the war; it was an ability to let my emotions be stirred by only one thing – my love for Helga. This concentration of my emotions on so small an area had begun as a young lover's happy illusion, had developed into a device to keep me from going insane during the war, and had finally become the permanent axis about which my thoughts revolved.

And so, with my Helga presumed dead, I became a death-worshipper, as content as any narrow-minded religious nut anywhere. Always alone, I drank toasts to her, said good morning to her, said good night to her, played music for her, and didn't give a damn for one thing else.

And then one day in 1958, after thirteen years of living like that, I bought a war-surplus wood-carving set. It was surplus not from the Second World War but from the Korean war. It cost me three dollars.

When I got it home, I started to carve up my broom handle to no particular purpose. And it suddenly occurred to me to make a chess set.

I speak of suddenness here, because I was startled to find myself with an enthusiasm. I was so enthusiastic that I carved for twelve hours straight, sank sharp tools into the palm of my left hand a dozen times, and still would not stop. I was an elated, gory mess when I was finished. I had a handsome set of chessmen to show for my labors.

And yet another strange impulse came upon me.

I felt compelled to show somebody, somebody still among the living, the marvelous thing I had made.

So, made boisterous by both creativity and drink, I went

downstairs and banged on the door of my neighbor, not even knowing who my neighbor was.

My neighbor was a foxy old man named George Kraft. That was only one of his names. The real name of this old man was Colonel Iona Potapov. This antique sonofabitch was a Russian agent, had been operating continuously in America since 1935.

I didn't know that.

And he didn't know at first who I was, either.

It was dumb luck that brought us together. No conspiracy was involved at first. It was I who knocked on his door, invaded his privacy. If I hadn't carved that chess set, we never would have met.

Kraft – and I'll call him that from now on, because that's how I think of him – had three or four locks on his front door.

I induced him to unlock them all by asking him if he played chess. There was dumb luck again. Nothing else would have made him open up.

People helping me with my research later, incidentally, tell me that the name of Iona Potapov was a familiar one in European chess tournaments in the early thirties. He actually beat the Grand Master Tartakover in Rotterdam in 1931.

When he opened up, I saw that he was a painter. There was an easel in the middle of his living room with a fresh canvas on it, and there were stunning paintings by him on every wall.

When I talk about Kraft, alias Potapov, I'm a lot more comfortable than when I talk about Wirtanen, alias God-knows-what. Wirtanen has left no more of a trail than an inchworm crossing a billiard table. Evidences of Kraft are everywhere. At this very moment, I'm told, Kraft's paintings are bringing as much as ten thousand dollars apiece in New York.

I have at hand a clipping from the New York *Herald Tribune* of March third, about two weeks ago, in which a critic says of Kraft as a painter:

Here at last is a capable and grateful heir to the fantastic inventiveness and experimentation in painting during the past hundred years. Aristotle is said to have been the last man to understand the whole of his culture. George Kraft is surely the first man to understand the whole of modern art – to understand it in his sinews and bones.

With incredible grace and firmness he combines the visions of a score of warring schools of painting, past and present. He thrills and humbles us with harmony, seems to say to us, 'If you want another Renaissance, this is what the paintings expressing its spirit will look like.'

George Kraft, alias Iona Potapov, is being permitted to continue his remarkable art career in the Federal Penitentiary at Fort Leavenworth. We all might well reflect, along, no doubt, with Kraft-Potapov himself, on how summarily his career would have been crushed in a prison in his native Russia.

Well – when Kraft opened his door for me, I knew his paintings were good. I didn't know they were that good. I suspect that the review above was written by a pansy full of brandy Alexanders.

'I didn't know I had a painter living underneath me,' I said to Kraft.

'Maybe you don't have one,' he said.

'Marvelous paintings!' I said. 'Where do you exhibit?'

'I never have,' he said.

'You'd make a fortune if you did,' I said.

'You're nice to say so,' he said, 'but I started painting too late.' He then told me what was supposed to be the story of his life, none of it true.

He said he was a widower from Indianapolis. As a young man, he said, he'd wanted to be an artist, but he'd gone into business instead – the paint and wallpaper business.

'My wife died two years ago,' he said, and he managed to look a little moist around the eyes. He had a wife, all right, but not underground in Indianapolis. He had a very live wife named Tanya in Borisoglebsk. He hadn't seen her for twenty-five years.

'When she died,' he said to me, 'I found my spirit wanted to choose between only two things – suicide, or the dreams I'd had in my youth. I am an old fool who borrowed the dreams of a young fool. I bought myself some canvas and paint, and I came to Greenwich Village.'

'No children?' I said.

'None,' he said sadly. He actually had three children and nine grandchildren. His oldest son, Ilya, is a famous rocket expert.

'The only relative I've got in this world is art –' he said, 'and I'm the poorest relative art ever had.' He didn't mean he was impoverished. He meant he was a bad painter. He had plenty of money, he told me. He'd sold his business in Indianapolis, he said, for a very good price.

'Chess –' he said, 'you said something about Chess?'

I had the chessmen I'd whittled, in a shoebox. I showed them to him. 'I just made these,' I said, 'and now I've got a terrific yen to play with them.'

'Pride yourself on your game, do you?' he said.

'I haven't played for a good while,' I said.

Almost all the chess I'd played had been with Werner Noth, my father-in-law, the Chief of Police of Berlin. I used to beat Noth pretty consistently – on Sunday afternoons when my Helga and I went calling on him. The only tournament I ever played in was an intramural thing in the German Ministry for Popular Enlightenment and Propaganda. I finished eleventh in a field of sixty-five.

In ping-pong I did a good deal better. I was ping-pong champion of the Ministry for four years running, singles and doubles. My doubles partner was Heinz Schildknecht, an expert at propagandizing Australians and New Zealanders. One time Heinz and I took on a doubles team composed of *Reichsleiter* Goebbels and *Oberdienstleiter* Karl Hederich. We sat them down 21–2, 21–1, 21–0.

History often goes hand-in-hand with sports.

Kraft had a chessboard. We set up my men on it, and we began to play.

And the thick, bristly, olive-drab cocoon I had built for myself was frayed a little, was weakened enough to let some pale light in.

I enjoyed the game, was able to come up with enough intuitively interesting moves to give my new friend entertainment while he beat me.

After that, Kraft and I played at least three games a day, every day for a year. And we built up between ourselves a pathetic sort of domesticity that we both felt need of. We began tasting our food again, making little discoveries in grocery stores, bringing them home to share. When strawberries came in season, I remember, Kraft and I whooped it up as though Jesus had returned.

One particularly touching thing between us was the matter of wines. Kraft knew a lot more than I did about wines, and he often brought home cobwebby treasures to go with a meal. But, even though Kraft always had a filled glass before him when we sat down to eat, the wine was all for me. Kraft was an alcoholic. He could not take so much as a sip of wine without starting on a bender that could last a month.

That much of what he told me about himself was true. He was a member of Alcoholics Anonymous, had been for sixteen years. While he used meetings as spy drops, his appetite for what the meetings offered spiritually was real. He once told me, in all sincerity, that the greatest contribution America had made to the world, a contribution that would be remembered for thousands of years, was the invention of the A.A.

It was typical of his schizophrenia as a spy that he should use an institution he so admired for purposes of espionage.

It was typical of his schiziphrenia as a spy that he should also be a true friend of mine, and that he should eventually think of a way to use me cruelly in advancing the Russian cause.

For a little while I lied to Kraft about who I was and what I'd done. But the friendship deepened so much, so fast, that I soon told him everything.

'It's so unjust!' he said. 'It makes me ashamed to be an American! Why can't the Government step forward and say, "Here! This man you've been spitting on is a hero!"'' He was indignant, and, for all I know, he was sincere in his indignation.

'Nobody spits on me,' I said. 'Nobody even knows I'm alive any more.'

He was eager to see my plays. When I told him I didn't have copies of any of them, he made me tell him about them, scene by scene – had me performing them for him.

He said he thought they were marvelous. Maybe he was sincere. I don't know. My plays seemed vapid to me, but it's possible he liked them.

What excited him, I think, was the idea of art, and not what I'd done with it.

'The arts, the arts, the arts –' he said to me one night. 'I don't know why it took me so long to realize how important they are. As a young man, I actually held them in supreme contempt. Now, whenever I think about them, I want to fall on my knees and weep.'

It was late autumn. Oysters had come back in season, and we were feasting on a dozen apiece. I'd known Kraft about a year then.

'Howard –' he said to me, 'future civilizations – better civilizations than this one – are going to judge all men by the extent to which they've been artists. You and I, if some future archaeologist finds our works miraculously preserved in some city dump, will be judged by the quality of our creations. Nothing else about us will matter.'

'Um,' I said.

'You've got to write again,' he said. 'Just as daisies bloom as daisies and roses bloom as roses – you must bloom as a writer and I must bloom as a painter. Everything else about us is uninteresting.'

'Dead men don't usually write very well,' I said.

'You're not dead!' he said. 'You're full of ideas. You can talk for hours on end.'

'Blather,' I said.

'Not blather!' he said hotly. 'All you need in this world to get writing again, writing better than ever before, is a woman.'

'A what?' I said.

'A woman,' he said.

'Where did you get this peculiar idea –' I said, 'from eating oysters? If you'll get one, I'll get one,' I said. 'How's that?'

'I'm too old for one to do me any good,' he said, 'but you're not.' Again, trying to separate the real from the fake, I have to declare this conviction of the real. He was really earnest about wanting me to write again, was convinced that a woman could do the trick. 'I would almost go through the humiliation of trying to be a man to a woman,' he said, 'if you would take a woman, too.'

'I've got one,' I said.

'You had one once,' he said. 'There's a world of difference.'

'I don't want to talk about it,' I said.

'I'm going to talk about it all the same,' he said.

'Then talk away,' I said, getting up from the table. 'Be a matchmaker to your heart's content. I'm going down to see what goodies came in the mail today.'

He'd annoyed me, and I went down the stairs to my mailbox, simply to walk off my annoyance. I wasn't eager to see the mail. I often went a week or more without seeing if I had any. The only things that were ever in my mailbox were dividend checks, notices of stockholders' meetings, trash mail addressed to 'Boxholder,' and advertising flyers for books and apparatus said to be useful in the field of education.

How did I happen to receive advertisements for educational

materials? One time I applied for a job as a teacher of German in a private school in New York. That was in 1950 or so.

I didn't get the job, and I didn't want it, either. I applied, I think, simply to demonstrate to myself that there really was such a person as me.

The application form I filled out was necessarily full of lies, was such a fabric of mendacity that the school did not even bother to tell me that I was unacceptable. Be that as it may, my name somehow found its way onto a list of those supposedly in teaching. Thereafter, flyers without end flew in.

I opened my mailbox on an accumulation of three or four days.

There was a check from Coca-Cola, a notice of a General Motors stockholders' meeting, a request from Standard Oil of New Jersey that I approve a new stock-option plan for my executives, and an ad for an eight-pound weight disguised to look like a schoolbook.

Object of the weight to give schoolchildren something to exercise with, in between classes. The ad pointed out that the physical fitness of American children was below that of the children of almost every land on earth.

But the ad for that queer weight wasn't the queerest thing in my mailbox. There were some things a lot queerer than that.

One was from the Francis X. Donovan Post of the Amercan Legion in Brookline, Massachusetts, a letter in a legal-size envelope.

Another was a tiny newspaper rolled tight and mailed from Grand Central Station.

I opened the newspaper first, found it to be *The White Christian Minuteman*, a scabrous, illiterate, anti-Semitic, anti-Negro, anti-Catholic hate sheet published by the Reverend Doctor Lionel J. D. Jones, D.D.S. 'Supreme Court,' said the biggest headline, 'Demands U.S. Be Mongrel!'

The second biggest headline said: 'Red Cross Gives Whites Negro Blood!'

These headlines could hardly startle me. They were, after

all, the sort of thing I had said for a living in Germany. Even closer to the spirit of the old Howard W. Campbell, Jr., actually, was the headline of a small story in one corner of the front page, a story titled: 'International Jewry Only Winners of World War II.'

I now opened the letter from the American Legion Post. It said:

Dear Howard:

I was very surprised and disappointed to hear you weren't dead yet. When I think of all the good people who died in World War Two, and then think that you're still alive and living in the country you betrayed, it makes me want to throw up. You will be happy to know that our Post resolved unanimously last night to demand that you either get hanged by the neck until dead or get deported back to Germany, which is the country you love so much.

Now that I know where you are, I will be paying you a call real soon. It will be nice to talk over old times.

When you go to sleep tonight, you smelly rat, I hope you dream of the concentration camp at Ohrdruf. I should have pushed you into a lime pit when I had the chance.

Very, very truly yours,
Bernard B. O'Hare
Post Americanism Chairman

Carbon copies to:

J. Edgar Hoover, F.B.I., Washington, D.C. Director, Central Intelligence Agency, Washington, D.C.

Editor, *Time*, New York City

Editor, *Newsweek*, New York City

Editor, *Infantry Journal*, Washington, D.C.

Editor, *The Legion Magazine*, Indianapolis, Indiana

Chief Investigator, House Un-American Activities
Committee, Washington, D.C.

Editor, *The White Christian Minuteman*, 395 Bleecker
St., New York City

Bernard B. O'Hare, of course, was the young man who had
captured me at the end of the war, who had frog-walked me
through the death camp at Ohrdruf, who had joined me in a
memorable photograph on the cover of *Life*.

When I found the letter from him in my mailbox in Greenwich Village, I was puzzled as to how he'd found out where
I was.

I leafed through *The White Christian Minuteman*, found
out O'Hare wasn't the only person who had rediscovered Howard W. Campbell, Jr. On page three of the *Minuteman*, under
a headline that said simply, 'American Tragedy!,' was this
brief tale:

> Howard W. Campbell, Jr., a great writer and one of
> the most fearless patriots in American history, now lives
> in poverty and loneliness in the attic of 27 Bethune Street.
> Such is the fate of thinking men brave enough to tell the
> truth about the conspiracy of international Jewish bank-
> ers and international Jewish Communists who will not
> rest until the bloodstream of every American is hope-
> lessly polluted with Negro and/or Oriental blood.

13 : The Reverend Doctor Lionel Jason
David Jones, D.D.S.,D.D. . . .

I am indebted to the Haifa Institute for the Documentation of War Criminals for the source material that makes it possible for me to include in this account a biography of Dr. Jones, publisher of *The White Christian Minuteman*.

Jones, though subject to no prosecution as a war criminal, has a very fat dossier. Leafing through that treasure house of souvenirs, I find these things to be true:

The Reverend Doctor Lionel Jason David Jones, D.D.S., D.D., was born in Haverhill, Massachusetts, in 1889, was raised as a Methodist.

He was the youngest son of a dentist, the grandson of two dentists, brother of two dentists, and the brother-in-law of three dentists. He himself set out to be a dentist, but was expelled from the Dental School of the University of Pittsburgh in 1910, for what would now be diagnosed, most likely, as paranoia. In 1910, he was dismissed for simple scholastic failure.

The syndrome of his failure was anything but simple. His examination papers were quite probably the longest such papers ever written in the history of dental education, and probably the most irrelevant as well. They began, sanely enough, with whatever subject the examination required Jones to discuss. But, regardless of that subject, Jones managed to go from it to a theory that was all his own – that the teeth of Jews and Negroes proved beyond question that both groups were degenerate.

His dental work was of a high order, so the faculty hoped to see him outgrow his political interpretations of teeth. But his case grew worse, until his examinations became frantic pamphlets, warning all Protestant Anglo-Saxons to unite against Jewish-Negro domination.

When Jones began to detect proof of degeneracy in the teeth of Catholics and Unitarians, and when five loaded pistols and a bayonet were found under his mattress, Jones was finally given the old heave-ho.

Jones' parents disowned him, which is something my parents never quite did to me.

Penniless, Jones found work as an apprentice embalmer in the Scharff Brothers Funeral Home in Pittsburgh. He became manager of the home within two years. A year after that, he married the widowed owner, Hattie Scharff. Hattie was fifty-eight at the time, and Jones was twenty-four. The many investigators into Jones' life, unfriendly investigators almost to a man, have been bound to conclude that Jones really loved his Hattie. The marriage, which endured until the death of Hattie in 1928, was a happy one.

In fact, it was so happy, so whole, so self-sufficient a nation of two that Jones did almost nothing during that time by way of alerting the Anglo-Saxons. He seems to have been content to confine his remarks on racial matters to workroom jests about certain cadavers, jests that would have seemed workaday in the most liberal of embalming establishments. And the years were golden, not only emotionally and financially, but creatively as well. Working with a chemist named Dr. Lomar Horthy, Jones developed Viverine, an embalming fluid, and Gingiva-Tru, a wonderfully life-like, gum-simulating substance for false teeth.

When Jones' wife died, Jones felt the need to be reborn. He was reborn a thing he had been latently all along. Jones became the sort of racial agitator who is spoken of as having crawled out from under a rock. Jones crawled out from under his rock in 1928. He sold his funeral home for eighty-four thousand dollars, and he founded *The White Christian Minuteman*.

Jones was wiped out by the stock market crash in 1929. His paper suspended publication after fourteen issues. The fourteen issues had been mailed free to every person in *Who's Who*. The only illustrations were photographs and diagrams of teeth, and every article was an explanation of some current events in terms of Jones' theories about dentition and race.

In the next-to-the-last issue, Jones billed himself on the masthead as, 'Dr. Lionel J. D. Jones, D.D.S.'

Penniless again, now forty years of age, Jones answered an ad in a funeral-home trade journal. An embalming school in Little Rock, Arkansas, needed a president. The ad was signed by the widow of the former president and owner.

Jones got the job, and the widow, too. The widow's name was Mary Alice Shoup. She was sixty-eight when Jones married her.

And Jones again became a devoted husband, a happy, whole, and quiet man.

The school he headed was named, straightforwardly enough, The Little Rock School of Embalming. It was losing eight thousand dollars a year. Jones took it out of the high-overhead field of embalming education, sold its real estate, and had it rechartered as The Western Hemisphere University of the Bible. The university held no classes, taught nothing, did all its business by mail. Its business was the awarding of doctorates in the field of divinity, framed and under glass, for eighty dollars a throw.

And Jones helped himself to a W.H.U.B. degree, out of open stock, so to speak. When his second wife died, when he brought out *The White Christian Minuteman* again, he appeared on the masthead as, 'The Reverend Doctor Lionel J. D. Jones, D.D.S., D.D.'

And he wrote and published at his own expense a book that combined not only dentistry and theology, but the fine arts as well. The name of the book was *Christ Was Not a Jew*. He proved his point by reproducing in the book fifty famous paintings of Jesus. According to Jones, not one painting showed Jewish jaws or teeth.

The first issues in the new series of *The White Christian Minuteman* were as unreadable as those of the old series. But then a miracle happened. The *Minuteman* jumped from four pages to eight. The make-up, the typography and the paper became snappy and handsome. Dental diagrams were replaced by newsy photographs, and the pages crackled with datelines and bylines from all over the world.

The explanation was simple – and obvious. Jones had been recruited and financed as a propaganda agent for Hitler's then-rising Third German Reich. Jones' news, photographs, cartoons and editorials were coming straight from the Nazi propaganda mills in Erfurt, Germany.

It is quite possible, incidentally, that much of his more scurrilous material was written by me.

Jones continued as a German propaganda agent even after the United States of America entered the Second World War. He wasn't arrested until July in 1942, when he was indicted with twenty-seven others for:

> Conspiring to destroy the morale and faith and confidence of the members of the military and naval forces of the United States and the people of the United States in their public officials and republican form of government; conspiring to seize upon and use and misuse the right of freedom of speech and of the press to spread their disloyal doctrines, intending and believing that any nation allowing its people the right of freedom of speech is powerless to defend itself against enemies masquerading as patriotic; and seeking to obstruct, impede, break down and destroy the proper functioning of its republican form of government under the guise of honest criticism; conspiring to render the Government of the United States bereft of the faith and confidence of the members of the military and naval forces and of the people, and thereby render that government powerless to defend the nation or the people against armed attack from without or treachery from within.

Jones was convicted. He was sentenced to fourteen years, served eight. When he was freed from Atlanta in 1950, he was a wealthy man. Viverine, his embalming fluid, and Gingiva-Tru, his counterfeit gum substance for false teeth, had both come to dominate their respective markets.

In 1955, he resumed publication of *The White Christian Minuteman.*

Five years after that, a lively elder statesman of seventy-one, an alert old man with no regrets, the Reverend Doctor Lionel J. D. Jones, D.D.S., D.D., paid me a call.

Why should I have honored him with such a full-dress biography?

In order to contrast with myself a race-baiter who is ignorant and insane. I am neither ignorant nor insane.

Those whose orders I carried out in Germany were as ignorant and insane as Dr. Jones. I knew it.

God help me, I carried out their instructions anyway.

Jones paid me a call a week after I found out how upsetting the contents of my mailbox had become. I tried to call on him first. He published his vile newspaper only a few blocks away from my attic, and I went there to beg him to retract the story.

He was not in.

When I got home, there was plenty of new mail in my mailbox, almost all of it from subscribers to *The White Christian Minuteman*. The common theme was that I was not alone, was not friendless. A woman in Mount Vernon, New York, told me there was a throne in Heaven for me. A man in Norfolk said I was the new Patrick Henry. A woman in St. Paul sent me two dollars to continue my good work. She apologized. She said that was all the money she had. A man in Bartlesville, Oklahoma, asked me why I didn't get out of Jew York and come live in God's country.

I didn't have any idea how Jones had found out about me.

Kraft claimed to be mystified, too. He wasn't really mystified. He had written to Jones as an anonymous fellow-patriot, telling him the glad news that I was alive. He had also asked that Jones send a complimentary copy of his great paper to Bernard B. O'Hare of the Francis X. Donovan Post of the American Legion.

Kraft had plans for me.

And he was, at the very same time, doing a portrait of me that surely showed more sympathetic insight into me, more intuitive affection than could ever have been produced by a wish to fool a boob.

I was sitting for the portrait when Jones came calling. Kraft had spilled a quart of turpentine. I opened the door to get rid of the fumes.

And a very strange chant came floating up the stairwell and through the open door.

I went out onto the landing outside the door, looked down the oak and plaster snail of the stairwell. All I could see was the hands of four persons – hands moving up the bannister.

The group was composed of Jones and three friends.

The curious chant went with the advance of the hands. The hands would move about four feet up the bannister, stop, and then the chant would come.

The chant was a panted count to twenty. Two of Jones' party, his bodyguard and his male secretary, had very bad hearts. To keep their poor old hearts from bursting, they were pausing every few steps, timing their rests by counting to twenty.

Jones' bodyguard was August Krapptauer, former *Vice-Bundesfuehrer* of the German-American *Bund*. Krapptauer was sixty-three, had done eleven years in Atlanta, was about to drop dead. But he still looked garishly boyish, as though he went to a mortuary cosmetologist regularly. The greatest achievement of his life was the arrangement of a joint meeting of the Bund and the Ku Klux Klan in New Jersey in 1940. At that meeting, Krapptauer declared that the Pope was a Jew and that the Jews held a fifteen-million-dollar mortgage on the Vatican. A change of Popes and eleven years in a prison laundry had not changed his mind.

Jones' secretary was an unfrocked Paulist Father named Patrick Keeley. 'Father Keeley,' as his employer still called him, was seventy-three. He was a drunk. He had, before the Second World War, been chaplain of a Detroit gun club which, as later came out, had been organized by agents of Nazi Germany. The dream of the club, apparently, was to shoot the Jews. One of Father Keeley's prayers at a club meeting was taken down by a newspaper reporter, was printed in full the next morning. The prayer appealed to so vicious and bigoted a God that it attracted the astonished attention of Pope Pius XI.

Keeley was unfrocked, and Pope Pius sent a long letter to the American Hierarchy in which he said, among other things: 'No true Catholic will take part in the persecution of his Jewish compatriots. A blow against the Jews is a blow against our common humanity.'

Keeley never went to prison, though many of his close friends did. While his friends enjoyed steam heat, clean beds and regular meals at government expense, Keeley shivered and itched and starved and drank himself blind on skid rows across the land. He would have been on a skid row still, or in a pauper's grave, if Jones and Krapptauer hadn't found and rescued him.

Keeley's famous prayer, incidentally, was a paraphrase of a satiric poem I had composed and delivered on short wave before. And, while I am setting the record straight as to my contributions to literature, may I point out that Vice-Bundes-fuehrer Krapptauer's claims about the Pope and the mortgage on the Vatican were my inventions, too.

So up the stairs these people came to see me, chanting, 'One, two, three, four. . . .'

And, slow as their progress was, the fourth member of the party lagged far behind.

The fourth member was a woman. All I could see of her was her pale and ringless hand.

The hand of Jones was in the lead. It glittered with rings like the hand of a Byzantine prince. An inventory of the jewelry on that hand would have revealed two wedding rings, a star-sapphire presented to him by the Mothers' Auxiliary of the Paul Revere Association of Militant Gentiles in 1940, a diamond swastika on an onyx field presented to him in 1939 by Baron Manfred Freiherr von Killinger, then German Consul General of San Francisco, and an American eagle carved in jade and mounted in silver, a piece of Japanese craftsman-ship, a present from Robert Sterling Wilson. Wilson was 'The Black Fuehrer of Harlem,' a colored man who went to prison in 1942 as a Japanese spy.

The jewelled hand of Jones left the bannister. Jones can-tered back down the stairs to the woman, said things to her I couldn't understand. And then up he came again, a remarkably sound-winded septuagenarian.

He came face to face with me, and he smiled showing me snow-white teeth set in Gingiva-Tru. 'Campbell?' he said, only a little out of breath.

'Yes,' I said.

'My name is Dr. Jones. I have a surprise for you,' he said.

'I've already seen your paper,' I said.

'No – not the paper,' he said. 'A bigger surprise than that.'

Father Keeley and Vice-Bundesfuehrer Krapptauer now came into view, wheezing, counting to twenty in shattered whispers.

'An even bigger surprise?' I said, preparing to square him away so savagely that he would never think of me as one of his own kind again.

'The woman I've brought with me –' he said.

'What about her?' I said.

'She's your wife,' he said.

'I got in touch with her –' said Jones, 'and she begged me not to tell you about her. She insisted it had to be like this, with her just walking in without any warning.'

'So I could see for myself if there was still room for me in your life,' said Helga. 'If there is no room, I will simply say goodbye again, disappear, and never bother you again.'

If the pale, ringless hand on the railing below was the hand of my Helga, it was the hand of a woman forty-five years old. It was the hand of a middle-aged woman who had been a prisoner of the Russians for sixteen years, if the hand was Helga's.

It was inconceivable that my Helga could still be lovely and gay.

If Helga had survived the Russian attack on the Crimea, had eluded all the crawling, booming, whistling, buzzing, creeping, clanking, bounding, chattering toys of war that killed quickly, a slower doom, a doom that killed like leprosy, had surely awaited her. There was no need for me to guess at the doom. It was well-known, uniformly applied to all women prisoners on the Russian front – was part of the ghastly routine of any thoroughly modern, thoroughly scientific, thoroughly asexual nation at thoroughly modern war.

If my Helga had survived the battle, her captors had surely prodded her with gun muzzles into a labor gang. They had surely shepherded her into one of Mother Russia's countless huddles of squinting, lumpy, hopeless, grubbing ragbags – had surely made of my Helga a digger of root crops in frosty fields, a lead-footed, splay-fingered clearer of rubble, a nameless, sexless dragger of noisy carts.

'My wife?' I said to Jones. 'I don't believe you.'

'It's easy enough to prove I'm a liar, if I am a liar,' he said pleasantly. 'Have a look for yourself.'

My pace down the stairs was firm and regular.

Now I saw the woman.

She smiled up at me, raising her chin so as to show her features frankly, clearly.

Her hair was snow-white.

Aside from that, she was my Hega untouched by time.

Aside from that, she was as lithe and blooming as my Helga had been on our wedding night.

We cried, like babies, wrestled each other up the stairs to my attic.

As we passed Father Keeley and Vice-Bundesfuehrer Krapptauer, I saw that Keeley was crying. Krapptauer stood at attention, honoring the idea of an Anglo-Saxon family. Jones, further up the stairs, was radiant with pleasure in the miracle he had worked. He rubbed and rubbed his jewelled hands.

'My – my wife,' I said to my old friend Kraft, as Helga and I entered my attic.

And Kraft, trying to keep from crying, chewed the bit of his cold corncob pipe in two. He never did quite cry, but he was close to doing it – genuinely close to doing it, I think.

Jones, Krapptauer and Keeley followed us in. 'How is it,' I said to Jones, 'that it's you who gives me back my wife?'

'A fantastic coincidence –' said Jones. 'One day I learned that you were still alive. A month later I learned that your wife was still alive. What can I call a coincidence like that but the Hand of God?'

'I don't know,' I said.

'My paper has a small circulation in West Germany,' said Jones. 'One of my subscribers read about you, and he sent me a cable. He asked me if I knew your wife had just turned up as a refugee in West Berlin.'

'Why didn't he cable *me*?' I said. I turned to Helga.

'Sweetheart –' I said in German, 'why didn't *you* cable me?'

'We'd been apart so long – I'd been dead so long,' she said in English. 'I thought surely you'd built a new life, with no room in it for me. I'd hoped that.'

'My life is nothing but room for you,' I said. 'It could never be filled by anyone but you.'

'So much to say, so much to tell –' she said, melting against me. I looked down on her wonderingly. Her skin was soft and clear. She was amazingly well-preserved for a woman of forty-five.

What made her state of preservation even more remarkable was the story she now told of how she had spent the past fifteen years.

She was captured and raped in the Crimea, she said. She was shipped to the Ukraine by boxcar, was put to work in a labor gang.

'We were stumbling sluts,' she said, 'married to mud. When the war was over, nobody bothered to tell us. Our tragedy was permanent. No records were kept of us anywhere. We shuffled through ruined villages aimlessly. Anyone who had a menial, pointless job to do had only to wave us down and we would do it.'

She separated herself from me in order to tell her yarn with larger gestures. I wandered over to my front window to listen – listen while looking through dusty panes into the twigs of a birdless, leafless tree.

Drawn crudely in the dust of three window-panes were a swastika, a hammer and sickle, and the Stars and Stripes. I had drawn the three symbols weeks before, at the conclusion of an argument about patriotism with Kraft. I had given a hearty cheer for each symbol, demonstrating to Kraft the meaning of patriotism to, respectively, a Nazi, a Communist, and an American.

'Hooray, hooray, hooray,' I'd said.

On and on Helga spun her yarn, weaving a biography on the crazy loom of modern history. She escaped from the labor gang after two years, she said, was caught a day later by Asiatic half-wits with submachine guns and police dogs.

She spent three years in the prison, she said, and then she was sent to Siberia as an interpreter and file clerk in a huge prisoner-of-war camp. Eight thousand S.S. men were still held captive there, though the war had been over for years.

'I was there for eight years,' she said, 'mercifully hypnotized by simple routines. We kept beautiful records of all those prisoners, of all those meaningless lives behind barbed-wire. Those S.S. men, once so young and lean and vicious, were growing gray and soft and self-pitying –' she said, 'husbands without wives, fathers without children, shopkeepers without shops, tradesmen without trades.'

Thinking about the subdued S.S. men, Helga asked herself the riddle of the Sphinx. 'What creature walks in the morning on four feet, at noon on two, at evening on three?'

'Man,' said Helga, huskily.

She told of being repatriated – repatriated after a fashion. She was returned not to Berlin but to Dresden, in East Germany. She was put to work in a cigarette factory, which she described in oppressive detail.

One day she ran away to East Berlin, then crossed to West Berlin. Days after that she was winging to me.

'Who paid your way?' I said.

'Admirers of yours,' said Jones warmly. 'Don't feel you have to thank them. They feel they owe you a debt of gratitude they'll never be able to repay.'

'For what?' I said.

'For having the courage to tell the truth during the war,' said Jones, 'when everybody else was telling lies.'

Vice-Bundesfuehrer Krapptauer, on his own initiative, went down all those stairs to get my Helga's luggage from Jones' limousine. The reunion of Helga and me had made him feel young and courtly again.

Nobody knew what he was up to until he reappeared in my doorway with a suitcase in either hand. Jones and Keeley were filled with consternation, because of Krapptauer's syncopated, leaky old heart.

The Vice-Bundesfuehrer was the color of tomato juice.

'You fool,' said Jones.

'No, no – I'm perfectly fine,' said Krapptauer, smiling.

'Why didn't you let Robert do it?' said Jones. Robert was his chauffeur, sitting in the limousine below. Robert was a colored man, seventy-three years old. Robert was Robert Sterling Wilson, erstwhile jailbird, Japanese agent, and 'Black Fuehrer of Harlem.'

'You should have let Robert bring those things up,' said Jones. 'My gosh – you mustn't risk your life like that.'

'It is an honor to risk my life,' said Krapptauer, 'for the wife of a man who served Adolf Hitler as well as Howard Campbell did.'

And he dropped dead.

We tried to revive him, but he was stone dead, slack-mouthed, obscenely gaga.

I ran down to the second floor, where Dr. Abraham Epstein lived with his mother. The doctor was home. Dr. Epstein treated poor old Krapptauer pretty roughly, forced him to demonstrate for us all how really dead he was.

Epstein was Jewish, and I thought Jones or Keeley might say something to him about the ways he was punching and poking Krapptauer. But the two antique Fascists were childishly respectful and dependent.

About the only thing Jones said to Epstein, after Epstein

had pronounced Krapptauer very dead, was, 'I happen to be a dentist, Doctor.'

'That so?' said Epstein. He wasn't much interested. He went back to his own apartment to call an ambulance.

Jones covered Krapptauer with one of my war-surplus blankets. 'Just when things were finally beginning to look up for him again,' he said of the death.

'In what way?' I said.

'He was beginning to get a little organization going again,' said Jones. 'Not a big thing – but loyal, dependable, devoted.'

'What was it called?' I said.

'The Iron Guard of the White Sons of the American Constitution,' said Jones. 'He had a real talent for welding perfectly ordinary youths into disciplined, determined force.' Jones shook his head sadly. 'He was getting such a fine response from the young people.'

'He loved young people, and young people loved him,' said Father Keeley. He was still weeping.

'That's the epitaph that should be carved on his tombstone,' said Jones. 'He used to work with youngsters in my cellar. You should see how he fixed it up for them – just ordinary kids from all walks of life.'

'Kids who would ordinarily be at loose ends and getting into trouble,' said Father Keeley.

'He was one of the greatest admirers you ever had,' Jones said to me.

'He was?' I said.

'Back when you were broadcasting, he never missed listening to you. When he went to prison, the first thing he did was build a short-wave receiver, just so he could go on listening to you. Every day he was bubbling over with the things you'd said the night before.'

'Um,' I said.

'You were a beacon, Mr. Campbell,' said Jones passionately. 'Do you realize what a beacon you were through all those black years?'

'Nope,' I said.

'Krapptauer had hoped you'd be the Idealism Officer for the Iron Guard,' said Jones.

'I'm the Chaplain,' said Keeley.

'Oh, who, who, who will lead the Iron Guard now?' said Jones. 'Who will step forward and pick up the fallen torch?'

There was a sharp, strong knock on the door. I opened the door, and outside stood Jones' chauffeur, a wrinkled old colored man with malevolent yellow eyes. He wore a black uniform with white piping, a Sam Browne belt, a nickel-plated whistle, a *Luftwaffe* hat without insignia, and black leather puttees.

There was no Uncle Tom in this cotton-haired old colored man. He walked in arthritically, but his thumbs were hooked into his Sam Browne belt, his chin was thrust out at us, and he kept his hat on.

'Everything all right up here?' he said to Jones. 'You was up here so long.'

'Not quite,' said Jones. 'August Krapptauer died.'

The Black Fuehrer of Harlem took the news in stride. 'All dying, all dying,' he said. 'Who's gonna pick up the torch when everybody's dead?'

'I just asked the same question myself,' said Jones. He introduced me to Robert.

Robert didn't shake hands. 'I heard about you,' he said, 'but I ain't never listened to you.'

'Well —' I said, 'you can't please all the people all of the time.'

'We was on opposite sides,' said Robert.

'I see,' I said. I didn't know anything about him, was agreeable to his belonging to any side that suited him.

'I was on the colored folks' side,' he said. 'I was with the Japanese.'

'Uh-huh,' I said.

'We needed you, and you needed us —' he said, speaking of the alliance between Germany and Japan in the Second World War. 'Only there was a lot of things we couldn't what you'd call agree about.'

'I guess that's so,' I said.

'I mean I heard you say you don't think the colored people was so good,' said Robert.

'Now, now,' said Jones soothingly. 'What useful purpose does it serve for us to squabble among ourselves? The thing to do is to pull together.'

'I just want to tell him what I tell you,' said Robert. 'I tell this Reverend gentleman here the same thing every morning, the same thing I tell you now. I give him his hot cereal for breakfast, and then I tell him: "The colored people are gonna rise up in righteous wrath, and they're gonna take over the world. White folks gonna finally lose!"'

'All right, Robert,' said Jones patiently.

'The colored people gonna have hydrogen bombs all their own,' he said. 'They working on it right now. Pretty soon gonna be Japan's turn to drop one. The rest of the colored folks gonna give them the honor of dropping the first one.'

'Where they going to drop it?' I said.

'China, most likely,' he said.

'On other colored people?' I said.

He looked at me pityingly. 'Who ever told you a Chinaman was a colored man?' he said.

Helga and I were finally left alone.

We were shy.

Being a man of fairly advanced years, so many of the years having been spent in celibacy, I was more than shy. I was afraid to test my strength as a lover. And the fear was amplified by the remarkable number of youthful characteristics my Helga had miraculously retained.

'This – this is what's known as getting to know each other again,' I said. Our conversation was in German.

'Yes,' she said. She had gone to the front window now, was looking at the patriotic devices I'd drawn on the dusty windowpanes. 'Which one of these is you now, Howard?' she said.

'Pardon me?' I said.

'The hammer and sickle, the swastika, or the Stars and Stripes –' she said, 'which one do you like the most?'

'Ask me about music,' I said.

'What?' she said.

'Ask me what kinds of music I like these days,' I said. 'I have some opinions on music. I have no political opinions at all.'

'I see,' she said. 'All right – what music do you like these days?'

' "White Christmas" –' I said, 'Bing Crosby's "White Christmas." '

'Excuse me?' she said.

'My favorite piece of music,' I said. 'I love it so much, I have twenty-six copies of it.'

She looked at me blankly. 'You do?' she said.

'It – it's a private joke,' I said lamely.

'Oh,' she said.

'Private –' I said. 'I've been living alone so long, everything about me's private. I'm surprised anyone's able to understand a word I say.'

'I will,' she said tenderly. 'Give me a little time – not much, but some – and I'll understand everything you say – again.' She shrugged. 'I have private jokes, too –'

'From now on –' I said, 'we'll make the privacy for two again.'

'That will be nice,' she said.

'Nation of two again,' I said.

'Yes,' she said. 'Tell me –'

'Anything at all,' I said.

'I know how Father died, but I haven't been able to find out a thing about Mother and Resi,' she said. 'Have you heard a word?'

'Nothing,' I said.

'When did you see them last?' she said.

I thought back, was able to give the exact date on which I'd last seen Helga's father, mother, and her pretty, imaginative little sister, Resi Noth.

'February 12, 1945,' I said, and I told her about that day.

That day was a day so cold that it made my bones ache. I stole a motorcycle, and I went calling on my in-laws, on the family of Werner Noth, the Chief of Police of Berlin.

Werner Noth lived on the outskirts of Berlin, well outside the target area. He lived with his wife and daughter in a walled white house that had the monolithic, earthbound grandeur of a Roman nobleman's tomb. In five years of total war, that house had not suffered so much as a cracked window-pane. Its tall, deep-set windows on the south framed an orchard within the walls. On the north they framed the jagged monuments in the ruins of Berlin.

I was wearing a uniform. At my belt was a tiny pistol and a big, fancy, ceremonial dagger. I didn't usually wear a uniform, but I was entitled to wear one – the blue and gold uniform of a Major in the Free American Corps.

The Free American Corps was a Nazi daydream – a daydream of a fighting unit composed mainly of American prisoners of war. It was to be a volunteer organization. It was to fight only on the Russian front. It was to be a high-morale fighting machine, motivated by a love of western civilization and a dread of the Mongol hordes.

When I call this unit a Nazi daydream, incidentally, I am suffering an attack of schizophrenia – because the idea of the Free American Corps began with me. I suggested its creation, designed its uniforms and insignia, wrote its creed.

That creed began, 'I, like my honored American forefathers, believe in true freedom –'

The Free American Corps was not a howling success. Only three American P.O.W.s joined. God only knows what became of them. I presume that they were all dead when I went calling on my in-laws, that I was the sole survivor of the Corps.

When I went calling, the Russians were only twenty miles from Berlin. I had decided that the war was almost over, that it was time for my career as a spy to end. I put on the uniform in order to dazzle any Germans who might try to keep me from getting out of Berlin. Tied to the back fender of my stolen motorcycle was a parcel of civilian clothes.

My call on the Noths had nothing to do with cunning. I really wanted to say goodbye to them, to have them say goodbye to me. I cared about them, pitied them – loved them in a way.

The iron gates of the great white house were open. Werner Noth himself was standing beside them, his hands on his hips. He was watching a work gang of Polish and Russian slave women. The women were lugging trunks and furniture from the house to three waiting horse-drawn wagons.

The wagon drivers were small, gold Mongols of some sort, early prizes of the Russian campaign.

The supervisor of the women was a fat, middle-aged Dutchman in a shabby business suit.

Guarding the women was a tall and ancient man with a single-shot rifle from the Franco-Prussian War.

On the old guard's ruined breast dangled the Iron Cross.

A woman slave shuffled out of the house carrying a luminously beautiful blue vase. She was shod in wooden clogs hinged with canvas. She was a nameless, ageless, sexless rag-bag. Her eyes were like oysters. Her nose was frostbitten, mottled white and cherry-red.

She seemed in danger of dropping the vase, of withdrawing so deeply into herself as simply to let the vase slip away.

My father-in-law saw the vase about to drop, and he went off like a burglar alarm. He shrieked at God to have pity on him just once, to make sense just once, to show him just one other energetic and intelligent human being.

He snatched the vase from the dazed woman. Close to unashamed tears, he asked us all to adore the blue vase that laziness and stupidity had almost let slip from the world.

The shabby Dutchman, the straw boss, now went up to the woman and repeated to her, word for word and shriek for shriek, what my father-in-law had said. The antique soldier came along with him, to represent the force that would be used on the woman, if necessary.

What was finally done with her was curious. She wasn't hurt.

She was deprived of the honor of carrying any more of Noth's things.

She was made to stand to one side while others continued to be trusted with treasures. Her punishment was to be made to feel like a fool. She had been given her opportunity to participate in civilization, and she had muffed it.

'I've come to say goodbye,' I said to Noth.

'Goodbye,' he said.

'I'm going to the front,' I said.

'Right over that way,' he said, pointing to the East. 'An easy walk from here. You can make it in a day, picking buttercups as you go.'

'It isn't very likely we'll see each other again, I guess,' I said.

'So?' he said.

I shrugged. 'So nothing,' I said.

'Exactly,' he said. 'Nothing and nothing and nothing.'

'May I ask where you're moving to?' I said.

'I am staying here,' he said. 'My wife and daughter are going to my brother's home outside of Cologne.'

'Is there anything I can do to help?' I said.

'Yes,' he said. 'You can shoot Resi's dog. It can't make the trip. I have no interest in it, will not be able to give it the care and companionship Resi has led it to expect. So shoot it, please.'

'Where is it?' I said.

'I think you'll find it in the music room with Resi,' he said. 'She knows it's to be shot. You will have no trouble with her.'

'All right,' I said.

'That's quite a uniform,' he said.

'Thank you,' I said.

'Would it be rude of me to ask what it represents?' he said. I had never worn it in his presence.

I explained it to him, showed him the device on the hilt of my dagger. The device, silver on walnut, was an American eagle that clasped a swastika in its right claw and devoured a snake in its left claw. The snake was meant to represent international Jewish communism. There were thirteen stars around the head of the eagle, representing the thirteen original American colonies. I had made the original sketch of the device, and, since I don't draw very well, I had drawn six-pointed stars of David rather than five-pointed stars of the U.S.A. The silversmith, while lavishly improving on my eagle, had reproduced my six-pointed stars exactly.

It was the stars that caught my father-in-law's fancy. 'These represent the thirteen Jews in Franklin Roosevelt's cabinet,' he said.

'That's a very funny idea,' I said.

'Everyone thinks the Germans have no sense of humor,' he said.

'Germany is the most misunderstood country in the world,' I said.

'You are one of the few outsiders who really understands us,' he said.

'I hope that's a compliment I deserve,' I said.

'It's a compliment you didn't come by very easily,' he said. 'You broke my heart when you married my daughter. I wanted a German soldier for a son-in-law.'

'Sorry,' I said.

'You made her happy,' he said.

'I hope so,' I said.

'That made me hate you more,' he said. 'Happiness has no place in war.'

'Sorry,' I said.

'Because I hated you so much,' he said, 'I studied you. I listened to everything you said. I never missed a broadcast.'

'I didn't know that,' I said.

'No one knows everything,' he said. 'Did you know,' he said, 'that until almost this very moment nothing would have delighted me more than to prove that you were a spy, to see you shot?'

'No,' I said.

'And do you know why I don't care now if you were a spy or not?' he said. 'You could tell me now that you were a spy, and we would go on talking calmly, just as we're talking now. I would let you wander off to wherever spies go when a war is over. You know why?' he said.

'No,' I said.

'Because you could never have served the enemy as well as you served us,' he said. 'I realized that almost all the ideas that I hold now, that make me unashamed of anything I may have felt or done as a Nazi, came not from Hitler, not from Goebbels, not from Himmler – but from you.' He took my hand. 'You alone kept me from concluding that Germany had gone insane.'

He turned away from me abruptly. He went to the oyster-eyed woman who had almost dropped the blue vase. She was standing against a wall where she had been ordered to stand, was numbly playing the punished dunce.

Werner Noth shook her a little, trying to arouse an atom of intelligence in her. He pointed to another woman who was carrying a hideous Chinese, carved-oak dog, carrying it as carefully as though it were a baby.

'You see?' Noth said to the dunce. He wasn't intentionally tormenting the dunce. He was trying to make her, in spite of her stupidity, a better-rounded, more useful human being.

'You see?' he said again, earnestly, helpfully, pleadingly. 'That's the way to handle precious things.'

19: Little Resi Noth...

I went into the music room of Werner Noth's emptying house and found little Resi and her dog.

Little Resi was ten years old then. She was curled in a wing-chair by a window. Her view was not of the ruins of Berlin but of the walled orchard, of the snowy lace that the treetops made.

There was no heat in the house. Resi was bundled up in a coat and scarf and thick wool stockings. A small suitcase was beside her. When the wagon train outside was ready to move, she would be ready to board it.

She had taken off her mittens, laid them neatly on the arm of the chair. She had bared her hands in order to pet the dog in her lap. The dog was a dachshund that had, on a wartime diet, lost all its hair and been all but immobilized by dropsical fat.

The dog looked like some early amphibian meant to waddle in ooze. While Resi caressed it, its brown eyes bugged with the blindness of ecstasy. Every bit of its awareness followed like thimbles the fingertips that stroked its hide.

I did not know Resi well. She had chilled me once, fairly early in the war, by lispingly calling me an American spy. Since then, I had spent as little time as possible before her childish gaze. When I came into the music room I was startled to see how much she was coming to resemble my Helga.

'Resi –?' I said.

She didn't look at me. 'I know,' she said. 'It's time to kill the dog.'

'It isn't anything I want to do very much,' I said.

'Are you going to do it,' she said, 'or are you going to give it to somebody to do?'

'Your father asked me to do it,' I said.

She turned to look at me. 'You're a soldier now,' she said.

'Yes,' I said.

'Did you put on your uniform just for killing the dog?' she said.

'I'm going to the front,' I said. 'I stopped by to say good-bye.'

'Which front?' she said.

'The Russians,' I said.

'You'll die,' she said.

'So I hear,' I said. 'Maybe not.'

'Everybody who isn't dead is going to be dead very soon now,' she said. She didn't seem to care much.

'Not everybody,' I said.

'I will be,' she said.

'I hope not,' I said. 'I'm sure you'll be fine,' I said.

'It won't hurt when I get killed,' she said. 'Just all of a sudden I won't be any more,' she said. She pushed the dog off her lap. It fell to the floor as passive as a *Knackwurst*.

'Take it,' she said. 'I never liked it anyway. I just felt sorry for it.'

I picked up the dog.

'It will be much better off dead,' she said.

'I think you're right,' I said.

'I'll be better off dead, too,' she said.

'That I can't believe,' I said.

'Do you want me to tell you something?' she said.

'All right,' I said.

'Since nobody's going to go on living much longer,' she said, 'I might as well tell you I love you.'

'That's very sweet,' I said.

'I mean really love you,' she said. 'When Helga was alive and you two would come here, I used to envy Helga. When Helga was dead, I started dreaming about how I would grow up and marry you and be a famous actress, and you would write plays for me.'

'I am honored,' I said.

'It doesn't mean anything,' she said. 'Nothing means anything. You go shoot the dog now.'

I bowed out, taking the dog with me. I took the dog out into the orchard, put it down in the snow, drew my tiny pistol.

Three people were watching me. One was Resi, who now stood at the music-room window. Another was the ancient soldier who was supposed to be guarding the Polish and Russian women.

The third was my mother-in-law, Eva Noth. Eva Noth stood at a second-story window. Like Resi's dog, Eva Noth had fattened dropsically on wartime food. The poor woman, made into sausage by unkind time, stood at attention, seemed to think that the execution of the dog was a ceremony of some nobility.

I shot the dog in the back of a neck. The report of my pistol was small, cheap, like the tinny spit of a B.B. gun.

The dog died without a shudder.

The old soldier came over, expressing a professional's interest in the sort of wound such a small pistol might make. He turned the dog over with his boot, found the bullet in the snow, murmured judiciously, as though I had done an interesting, instructive thing. He now began to talk of all sorts of wounds he had seen or heard of, all sorts of holes in once-living things.

'You're going to bury it?' he said.

'I suppose I'd better,' I said.

'If you don't,' he said, 'somebody will eat it.'

I found out only recently, in 1958 or 1959, how my father-in-law died. I knew he was dead. The detective agency I had hired to find word of Helga had told me that much – that Werner Noth was dead.

The details of his death came to hand by chance – in a Greenwich Village barber shop. I was leafing through a girly magazine, admiring the way women were made, and awaiting my turn for a haircut. The story advertised on the magazine cover was 'Hangwomen for the Hangman of Berlin.' There was no reason for me to suppose that the article was about my father-in-law. Hanging hadn't been his business. I turned to the article.

And I looked for quite a while at a murky photograph of Werner Noth being hanged from an apple tree without suspecting who the hanged man was. I looked at the faces of the people at the hanging. They were mostly women, nameless, shapeless ragbags.

And I played a game, counting the ways in which the magazine cover had lied. For one thing, the women weren't doing the hanging. Three scrawny men in rags were doing it. For another thing, the women in the photograph weren't beautiful, and the hangwomen on the cover were. The hangwomen on the cover had breasts like cantaloupes, hips like horse collars, and their rags were the pathetic remains of nightgowns by Schiaparelli. The women in the photograph were as pretty as catfish wrapped in mattress-ticking.

And then, just before I began to read the story of the hanging, I began, tentatively and queasily, to recognize the shattered building in the background. Behind the hangman, looking like a mouthful of broken teeth, was all that was left of the home of Werner Noth, of the home where my Helga had been raised as a good German citizen, of the home where I had said farewell to a ten-year-old nihilist named Resi.

I read the text.

The text was by a man named Ian Westlake, and it was very well done. Westlake, an Englishman, a liberated prisoner of war, had seen the hanging shortly after his liberation by the Russians. The photographs were his.

Noth, he said, had been hanged from his own apple tree by slave laborers, mostly Poles and Russians, quartered nearby. Westlake did not call my father-in-law 'The Hangman of Berlin.'

Westlake went to some trouble to find out what crimes Noth had committed, and he concluded that Noth had been no better and no worse than any other big city chief of police.

'Terror and torture were the provinces of other branches of the German police,' said Westlake. 'Werner Noth's own province was what is regarded in every big city as ordinary law and order. The force he directed was the sworn enemy of drunks, thieves, murderers, rapists, looters, confidence men, prostitutes, and other disturbers of the peace, and it did its best to keep the city traffic moving.

'Noth's principal offense,' said Westlake, 'was that he introduced persons suspected of misdemeanors and crimes into a system of courts and penal institutions that was insane. Noth did his best to distinguish between the guilty and the innocent, using the most modern police methods; but those to whom he handed over his prisoners found the distinction of no importance. Merely to be in custody, with or without trial, was a crime. Prisoners of every sort were all to be humiliated, exhausted and killed.'

Westlake went on to say that the slave laborers who hanged Noth had no clear idea who he was, beyond the fact that he was somebody important. They hanged him for the satisfaction of hanging somebody important.

Noth's house, said Westlake, had been demolished by Russian artillery, but Noth had continued to live in one undamaged room in the back. Westlake took an inventory of the room, found it to contain a bed, a table, and a candlestick. On the table were framed photographs of Helga, Resi, and Noth's wife.

There was a book. It was a German translation of *The Meditations of Marcus Aurelius*.

Why such a miserable magazine had bought such a fine piece of reporting was not explained. What the magazine was sure its readers would like was the description of the hanging itself.

My father-in-law was stood on a footstool four inches high. The rope was put around his neck and drawn tight over the limb of a budding apple tree. The footstool was then kicked out from under him. He could dance on the ground while he strangled.

Good?

He was revived eight times, and hanged nine.

Only after the eighth hanging were his last bits of courage and dignity gone. Only after the eighth hanging did he act like a child being tortured.

'For that performance,' said Westlake, 'he was rewarded with what he wanted most in all this world. He was rewarded with death. He died with an erection and his feet were bare.'

I turned the page of the magazine to see if there was more. There was more, but not more of the same. There was a full-page photograph of a pretty woman with her thighs spread wide and her tongue stuck out.

The barber called out to me. He shook another man's hair out of the cloth he was going to put around my neck.

'Next,' he said.

21: My Best Friend . . .

I've said that I'd stolen the motorcycle I rode when I called on Werner Noth for the last time. I should explain.

I didn't really steal it. I just borrowed it for all eternity from Heinz Schildknecht, my ping-pong doubles partner, my closest friend in Germany.

We used to drink together, used to talk long into the night, especially after we both lost our wives.

'I feel I can tell you anything – absolutely anything,' he said to me one night, late in the war.

'I feel the same way about you, Heinz,' I said.

'Anything I have is yours,' he said.

'Anything I have is yours, Heinz,' I said.

The amount of property between us was negligible. Neither one of us had a home. Our real estate and our furniture were blown to smithereens. I had a watch, a typewriter, and a bicycle, and that was about it. Heinz had long since traded his watch and his typewriter and even his wedding ring for black-market cigarettes. All he had left in this vale of tears, excepting my friendship and the clothes on his back, was a motor-cycle.

'If anything ever happens to the motorcycle,' he said to me, 'I am a pauper.' He looked around for eavesdroppers. 'I will tell you something terrible,' he said.

'Don't if you don't want to,' I said.

'I want to,' he said. 'You are the person I can tell terrible things to. I am going to tell you something simply awful.'

The place where we were drinking and talking was a pillbox near the dormitory where we both slept. It had been built very recently for the defense of Berlin, had been built by slaves. It wasn't armed, wasn't manned. The Russians weren't that close yet.

Heinz and I sat there with a bottle and a candle between us, and he told me the terrible thing. He was drunk.

'Howard —' he said, 'I love my motorcycle more than I loved my wife.'

'I want to be a friend of yours, and I want to believe everything you say, Heinz,' I said to him, 'but I refuse to believe that. Let's just forget you said it, because it isn't true.'

'No,' he said, 'this is one of those moments when somebody really speaks the truth, one of those rare moments. People hardly ever speak the truth, but now I am speaking the truth. If you are the friend I think you are, you'll do me the honor of believing the friend I think I am when I speak the truth.'

'All right,' I said.

There were tears streaming down his cheeks. 'I sold her jewelry, her favorite furniture, even her meat ration one time – all for cigarettes for me,' he said.

'We've all done things we're ashamed of,' I said.

'I would not quit smoking for her sake,' said Heinz.

'We all have bad habits,' I said.

'When the bomb hit the apartment, killed her and left me with nothing but a motorcycle,' he said, 'the black-market man offered me four thousand cigarettes for the motorcycle.'

'I know,' I said. He told me the same story every time he got drunk.

'And I gave up smoking at once,' he said, 'because I loved the motorcycle so.'

'We all cling to something,' I said.

'To the wrong things —' he said, 'and we start clinging too late. I will tell you the one thing I really believe out of all the things there are to believe.'

'All right,' I said.

'All people are insane,' he said. 'They will do anything at any time, and God help anybody who looks for reasons.'

As for the kind of woman Heinz's wife had been: I knew her only slightly, though I saw her fairly often. She was a non-stop talker, which made her hard to know, and her theme was always the same: successful people, people who saw opportunities and grasped them firmly, people who, unlike her husband, were important and rich.

'Young Kurt Ehrens –' she would say, 'only twenty-six, and a full colonel in the S.S.! And his brother Heinrich – he can't be more than thirty-four, but he has eighteen thousand foreign workers under him, all building tank traps. Heinrich knows more about tank traps than any man alive, they say, and I used to dance with him.'

On and on she would talk this way, with poor Heinz in the background, smoking his brains out. And one thing she did to me was make me deaf to all success stories. The people she saw as succeeding in a brave new world were, after all, being rewarded as specialists in slavery, destruction, and death. I don't consider people who work in those fields successful.

As the war drew to a close, Heinz and I couldn't drink in our pillbox any more. An eighty-eight was set up in it, and the gun was manned by boys about fifteen or sixteen years old. There was a success story for Heinz's late wife – boys that young, and yet with men's uniforms and a fully-armed death trap all their own.

So Heinz and I did our drinking and talking in our dormitory, a riding hall jammed with bombed-out government workers sleeping on straw mattresses. We kept our bottle hidden, since we did not care to share it.

'Heinz –' I said to him one night, 'I wonder how good a friend you really are.'

He was stung. 'Why should you ask me that?' he said.

'I want to ask a favor of you – a very big one – and I don't know if I should,' I said.

'I demand that you ask it!' he said.

'Lend me your motorcycle, so I can visit my in-laws tomorrow,' I said.

He did not hesitate, did not quail. 'Take it!' he said.

So the next morning I did.

We started out the next morning side by side, Heinz on my bicycle, me on his motorcycle.

I kicked the starter, put the motorcycle in gear, and off I went, leaving my best friend smiling in a cloud of blue exhaust.

Off I went – vroooom, ka-pow, kapow – vaaaaaaa-roooooom!

And he never saw his motorcycle or his best friend again.

I have asked the Haifa Institute for the Documentation of War Criminals if they have any news of Heinz, though he wasn't much of a war criminal. The Institute delights me with the news that Heinz is now in Ireland, is chief grounds-keeper for Baron Ulrich Werther von Schwefelbad. Von Schwefelbad bought a big estate in Ireland after the war.

The Institute tells me that Heinz is an expert on the death of Hitler, having stumbled into Hitler's bunker while Hitler's gasoline-soaked body was burning but still recognizable.

Hello, out there, Heinz, in case you read this.

I was really very fond of you, to the extent that I am capable of being fond of anybody.

Give the Blarney Stone a kiss for me.

What were you doing in Hitler's bunker – looking for your motorcycle and your best friend?

22 : The Contents of an Old Trunk ...

'Look,' I said to my Helga in Greenwich Village, after I had told her what little I knew about her mother, father, and sister, 'this attic will never do for a love nest, not even for one night. We'll get a taxi. We'll go to some hotel. And tomorrow we'll throw out all this furniture, get everything brand new. And then we'll look for a really nice place to live.'

'I'm very happy here,' she said.

'Tomorrow,' I said, 'we'll find a bed like our old bed – two miles long and three miles wide, with a headboard like an Italian sunset. Remember – oh Lord, remember?'

'Yes,' she said.

'Tonight in a hotel,' I said. 'Tomorrow night in a bed like that.'

'We leave right now?' she said.

'Whatever you say,' I said.

'Can I show you my presents first?' she said.

'Presents?' I said.

'For you,' she said.

'You're my present,' I said. 'What more would I want?'

'You might want these, too,' she said, freeing the catches on a suitcase. 'I hope you do.' She opened the suitcase, showed me that it was full of manuscripts. Her present to me was my collected works, my collected serious works, almost every heartfelt word ever written by me, the late Howard W. Campbell, Jr. There were poems, stories, plays, letters, one unpublished book – the collected works of myself as a buoyant, free, and young, young man.

'How queer this makes me feel,' I said.

'I shouldn't have brought them?' she said.

'I hardly know,' I said. 'These pieces of paper were me at one time.' I picked up the book manuscript, a bizarre experiment called *Memoirs of a Monogamous Casanova*. 'This you should have burned,' I said.

'I would just as gladly burn my own right arm,' she said.

I put the book aside, took up a sheaf of poems. 'What does this young stranger have to say about life?' I said, and I read a poem, a poem in German, aloud:

> *Kühl und hell der Sonnenaufgang,*
> *leis und süss der Glocke Klang.*
> *Ein Mägdlein hold, Krug in der Hand,*
> *sitzt an des tiefen Brunnens Rand.*

In English? Roughly:

> Cool, bright sunrise —
> Faint, sweet bell.
> Maiden with a pitcher
> By a cool, deep well.

I read that poem out loud, and then I read another. I was and am a very bad poet. I do not set down these poems to be admired. The second poem I read was, I think, the next-to-the-last poem I ever wrote. It was dated 1937, and it had this title: '*Gedanken über unseren Abstand vom Zeitgeschehen,*' or, roughly, 'Reflections on Not Participating in Current Events.'

It went like this:

> *Eine mächtige Dampfwalze naht*
> *und schwärzt der Sonne Pfad,*
> *rollt über geduckte Menschen dahin,*
> *will keiner ihr entfliehn.*
> *Mein Lieb und ich schaun starren Blickes*
> *das Rätsel dieses Blutgeschickes.*
> *'Kommt mit herab,' die Menschheit schreit,*
> *'Die Walze ist die Geschichte der Zeit!'*
> *Mein Lieb und ich gehn auf die Flucht,*
> *wo keine Dampfwalze uns sucht,*
> *und leben auf den Bergeshöhen,*
> *getrennt vom schwarzen Zeitgeschehen.*
> *Sollen wir bleiben mit den andern zu sterben?*
> *Doch nein, wir zwei wollen nicht verderben!*

Nun ist's vorbei! – Wir sehn mit Erbleichen
die Opfer der Walze, verfaulte Leichen.

In English?

> I saw a huge steam roller,
> It blotted out the sun.
> The people all lay down, lay down;
> They did not try to run.
> My love and I, we looked amazed
> Upon the gory mystery.
> 'Lie down, lie down!' the people cried,
> 'The great machine is history!'
> My love and I, we ran away,
> The engine did not find us.
> We ran up to a mountain top,
> Left history far behind us.
> Perhaps we should have stayed and died,
> But somehow we don't think so.
> We went to see where history'd been,
> And my, the dead did stink so.

'How is it,' I said to Helga, 'that you have all these things?'

'When I went to West Berlin,' she said, 'I went to the theater to see if there was a theater left – if there was anyone I knew left – if anyone had any news of you.' She didn't have to explain which theater she meant. She meant the little theater where my plays had been produced in Berlin, where Helga had been the star so often.

'It got through most of the war, I know,' I said. 'It still exists?'

'Yes,' she said. 'And when I asked about you, they knew nothing. And when I told them what you had once meant to that theater, someone remembered that there was a trunk in the loft with your name on it.'

I passed my hand over the manuscripts. 'And in it were these,' I said. I remembered the trunk now, remembered when

I'd closed it up at the start of the war, remembered when I'd thought of the trunk as a coffin for the young man I would never be again.

'You already have copies of these things?' she said.

'No,' I said. 'Not a scrap.'

'You don't write any more?' she said.

'There hasn't been anything I've wanted to say,' I said.

'After all you've seen, all you've been through, darling?' she said.

'It's all I've seen, all I've been through,' I said, 'that makes it damn nearly impossible for me to say anything. I've lost the knack of making sense. I speak gibberish to the civilized world, and it replies in kind.'

'There was another poem, your last poem, it must have been –' she said, 'written in eyebrow pencil on the inside of the trunk lid.'

'Oh?' I said.

She recited it for me:

> *Hier liegt Howard Campbells Geist geborgen,*
> *frei von des Körpers quälenden Sorgen.*
> *Sein leerer Leib durchstreift die Welt,*
> *und kargen Lohn dafür erhält.*
> *Triffst du die beiden getrennt allerwärts*
> *verbrenn den Leib, doch schone dies, sein Herz.*

In English?

> Here lies Howard Campbell's essence,
> Freed from his body's noisome nuisance.
> His body, empty, prowls the earth,
> Earning what a body's worth.
> If his body and his essence remain apart,
> Burn his body, but spare this, his heart.

There was a knock on the door.

It was George Kraft knocking on my door, and I let him in. He was very jangled because his corn-cob pipe had disappeared. It was the first time I'd seen him without the pipe, the first time he showed me how dependent he was on the pipe for peace. He was so full of anxiety that he whined.

'Somebody took it or somebody knocked it down behind something or – I just can't imagine why anybody would have done anything with it,' he whined. He expected Helga and me to share his anxiety, to think that the disappearance of the pipe was the most important event of the day.

He was insufferable.

'Why would anybody touch the pipe?' he said. 'What good would it do anybody?' He was opening and shutting his hands, blinking often, sniffling, acting like a dope addict with withdrawal symptoms, though he had never smoked anything in the missing pipe. 'Just tell me –' he said, 'why would anybody take the pipe?'

'I don't know, George,' I said testily. 'If we find it, we'll let you know.'

'Could I look around for myself?' he said.

'Go ahead,' I said.

And he turned the place upside down, rattling pots and pans, banging cupboard doors, fishing back of the radiators with a poker, clangingly.

The effect of this performance on Helga and me was to wed us – to urge us into an easy relationship that might otherwise have been a long while coming.

We stood side by side, resenting the invasion of our nation of two.

'It wasn't a very valuable pipe, was it?' I said.

'Yes it was – to me,' he said.

'Buy another one,' I said.

'I want *that* one,' he said. 'I'm used to it. That's the pipe I want.' He opened the breadbox, looked inside.

'Maybe the ambulance attendants took it,' I said.

'Why would they do that?' he said.

'Maybe they thought it belonged to the dead man,' I said. 'Maybe they put it in the dead man's pocket.'

'That's it!' cried Kraft, and he scuttled out the door.

One of the things Helga had in her suitcase, as I've already said, was a book by me. It was a manuscript. I had never intended that it be published. I regarded it as unpublishable – except by pornographers.

It was called *Memoirs of a Monogamous Casanova*. In it I told of my conquests of all the hundreds of women my wife, my Helga, had been. It was clinical, obsessed – some say, insane. It was a diary, recording day by day for the first two years of the war, our erotic life – to the exclusion of all else. There is not one word in it to indicate the century or the continent of its origin.

There is a man of many moods, a woman of many moods. In some of the early entries, settings are referred to sketchily. But from there on, there are no settings at all.

Helga knew I kept the peculiar diary. I kept it as one of many devices for keeping our sexual pleasure keen. The book is not only a report of an experiment, but a part of the experiment it reports – a self-conscious experiment by a man and a woman to be endlessly fascinating to each other sexually –

To be more than that.

To be to each other, body and soul, sufficient reasons for living, though there might not be a single other satisfaction to be had.

The epigraph of the book is to the point, I think.

It is a poem by William Blake called 'The Question Answered':

> What is it men in women do require?
> The lineaments of Gratified Desire.
> What is it women do in men require?
> The lineaments of Gratified Desire.

I might aptly add here one last chapter to the Memoirs, chapter 643, describing the night I spent in a New York hotel with Helga, after having been without her for so many years.

I leave it to an editor of taste and delicacy to abridge with innocent polka dots whatever might offend.

MEMOIRS OF A MONOGAMOUS CASANOVA, CHAPTER 643

We had been apart for sixteen years. My first lust that night was in my finger tips. Other parts of me ... that were contented later were contented in a ritual way, thoroughly, too ... clinical perfection. No part of me could complain, and no part of my wife could complain, I trust, of being victimized by busy-work, time-serving ... or jerry-building. But my finger tips had the best of it that night. . . .

Which is not to say that I found myself to be an ... old man, dependent, if I was to please a woman, on ... foreplay and nothing more. On the contrary, I was as ... ready a lover as a seventeen-year-old ... with his ... girl ...

And as full of wonder.

And it was in my fingers that the wonder lived. Calm, resourceful, thoughtful, these ... explorers, these ... strategists, these ... scouts, these ... skirmishers, deployed themselves over the ... terrain.

And all the news they gathered was good. . . .

My wife was a ... slave girl bedded with an ... emperor that night, seemingly struck dumb, seemingly not even able to speak a word of my language. And yet, how eloquent she was, letting her eyes, her breathing ... express what they must, unable to keep them from expressing what they must. . . .

And how simple, how sublimely familiar was the tale her ... body told! ... It was like the breeze's tale of what a breeze is, like the rose's tale of what the rose is. . . .

After my subtle, thoughtful and grateful fingers came greedier things, instruments of pleasure without memories, without manners, without patience. These my slave girl met in greedy kind ... until Mother Nature herself, who had made the most extravagant demands upon us, could ask no more. Mother Nature herself . . . called an end to the game. . . .

We rolled apart. . . .

We spoke coherently to each other for the first time since bedding down.

'Hello,' she said.

'Hello,' I said.

'Welcome home,' she said.

End of chapter 643.

The city sky was clean and hard and bright the next morning, looking like an enchanted dome that would shatter at a tap or ring like a great glass bell.

My Helga and I stepped from our hotel to the sidewalk snappily. I was lavish in my courtliness, and my Helga was no less grand in her respect and gratitude. We had had a marvelous night.

I was not wearing war-surplus clothing. I was wearing the clothes I had put on after fleeing Berlin, after shucking off the uniform of the Free American Corps. I was wearing the clothes – fur-collared impresario's cloak and blue serge suit – I had been captured in. I was also carrying, for whimsy, a cane. I did marvelous things with the cane: rococo manuals of arms, Charlie Chaplin twirls, polo strokes at orts in the gutter.

And all the while my Helga's small hand rested on my good left arm, creeping in an endless and erotic exploration of the tingling area between the inside of my elbow and the crest of my stringy biceps.

We were on our way to buy a bed, a bed like our bed in Berlin.

But all the stores were closed. The day wasn't Sunday, and it wasn't any holiday I could think of. When we got to Fifth Avenue, there were American flags flying as far as the eye could see. 'Good God Almighty,' I said wonderingly.

'What does it mean?' said Helga.

'Maybe they declared war last night,' I said.

She tightened her fingers on my arm convulsively. 'You don't really think so, do you?' she said. She thought it was possible.

'A joke,' I said. 'Some kind of holiday, obviously.'

'What holiday?' she said.

I was still drawing blanks. 'As your host in this wonderful land of ours,' I said, 'I should explain to you the deep significance of this great day in our national lives, but nothing comes to me.'

'Nothing?' she said.

'I'm as baffled as you are,' I said. 'I might as well be the Prince of Cambodia.'

A uniformed colored man was sweeping the walk in front of an apartment. His blue and gold uniform bore a striking resemblance to the uniform of the Free American Corps, even to the final touch of a pale lavender stripe down his trouser legs. The name of the apartment house was stitched over his breast pocket. 'Sylvan House' was the name of the place, though the only tree near it was a sapling, bandaged, armored and guy-wired.

I asked the man what day it was.

He told me it was Veterans' Day.

'What date is it?' I said.

'November eleventh, sir,' he said.

'November eleventh is Armistice Day, not Veterans' Day,' I said.

'Where you been?' he said. 'They changed all that years ago.'

'Veterans' Day,' I said to Helga as we walked on. 'Used to be Armistice Day. Now it's Veterans' Day.'

'That upsets you?' she said.

'Oh, it's just so damn cheap, so damn typical,' I said. 'This used to be a day in honor of the dead of World War One, but the living couldn't keep their grubby hands off of it, wanted the glory of the dead for themselves. So typical, so typical. Any time anything of real dignity appears in this country, it's torn to shreds and thrown to the mob.'

'You hate America, don't you?' she said.

'That would be as silly as loving it,' I said. 'It's impossible for me to get emotional about it, because real estate doesn't interest me. It's no doubt a great flaw in my personality, but I can't think in terms of boundaries. Those imaginary lines are as unreal to me as elves and pixies. I can't believe that they mark the end or the beginning of anything of real concern to a human soul. Virtues and vices, pleasures and pains cross boundaries at will.'

'You've changed so,' she said.

'People should be changed by world wars,' I said, 'else what are world wars for?'

'Maybe you've changed so much you don't really love me any more,' she said. 'Maybe I've changed so much —'

'After a night like last night,' I said, 'how could you say such a thing?'

'We really haven't talked anything over —' she said.

'What is there to talk about?' I said. 'Nothing you could say would make me love you more or less. Our love is too deep for words ever to touch it. It's soul love.'

She sighed. 'How lovely that is — if it's true.' She put her hands close together, but not touching. 'Our souls in love.'

'A love that can weather anything,' I said.

'Your soul feels love now for my soul?' she said.

'Obviously,' I said.

'And you couldn't be deceived by that feeling?' she said. 'You couldn't be mistaken?'

'Not a chance,' I said.

'And nothing I could say could spoil it?' she said.

'Nothing,' I said.

'All right,' she said, 'I have something to say that I was afraid to say before. I'm not afraid to say it now.'

'Say away!' I said lightly.

'I'm not Helga,' she said. 'I'm her little sister Resi.'

After she gave me the news, I took her into a nearby cafeteria so we could sit down. The ceiling was high. The lights were merciless. The clatter was hell.

'Why did you do this to me?' I said.

'Because I love you,' she said.

'How could you love me?' I said.

'I've always loved you – since I was a very little girl,' she said.

I put my head in my hands. 'This is terrible,' I said.

'I – I thought it was beautiful,' she said.

'What now?' I said.

'It can't go on?' she said.

'Oh, Jesus – how bewildering,' I said.

'I found the words to kill the love, didn't I –' she said, 'the love that couldn't be killed?'

'I don't know,' I said. I shook my head. 'What is this strange crime I've committed?'

'I'm the one who's committed the crime,' she said. 'I must have been crazy. When I escaped into West Berlin, when they gave me a form to fill out, asked me who I was, what I was – who I knew –'

'That long, long story you told –' I said, 'about Russia, about Dresden – was any of it true?'

'The cigarette factory in Dresden – that was true,' she said. 'My running away to Berlin was true. Not much else. The cigarette factory –' she said, 'that was the truest thing – ten hours a day, six days a week, ten years.'

'Sorry,' I said.

'I'm the one who's sorry,' she said. 'Life's been too hard for me ever to afford much guilt. A really bad conscience is as much out of my reach as a mink coat. Daydreams were what kept me going at that machine, day after day, and I had no right to them.'

'Why not?' I said.

'They were all daydreams of being somebody I wasn't.'

'No harm in that,' I said.

'Look at the harm,' she said. 'Look at you. Look at me. Look at our love affair. I daydreamed of being my sister Helga. Helga, Helga, Helga – that's who I was. The lovely actress with the handsome playwright husband, that's who I was. Resi, the cigarette machine operator – she simply disappeared.'

'You could have picked a worse person to be,' I said.

She became very brave now. 'It's who I am,' she said. 'It's who I am. I'm Helga, Helga, Helga. You believed it. What better test could I be put to? Have I been Helga to you?'

'That's a hell of a question to put to a gentleman,' I said.

'Am I entitled to an answer?' she said.

'You're entitled to the answer yes,' I said. 'I have to answer yes, but I have to say I'm not a well man, either. My judgment, my senses, my intuition obviously aren't all they could be.'

'Or maybe they are all they should be,' she said. 'Maybe you haven't been deceived.'

'Tell me what you know about Helga,' I said.

'Dead,' she said.

'You're sure?' I said.

'Isn't she?' she said.

'I don't know,' I said.

'I haven't heard a word,' she said. 'Have you?'

'No,' I said.

'Living people make words, don't they?' she said. 'Especially if they love someone as much as Helga loved you.'

'You'd think so,' I said.

'I love you as much as Helga did,' she said.

'Thank you,' I said.

'And you did hear from me,' she said. 'It took some doing, but you did hear from me.'

'Indeed,' I said.

'When I got to West Berlin,' she said, 'and they gave me the forms to fill out – name, occupation, nearest living relative – I had my choice. I could be Resi Noth, cigarette-machine operator, with no relatives anywhere. Or I could be Helga Noth, actress, wife of a handsome, adorable, brilliant playwright in the U.S.A.' She leaned forward. 'You tell me –' she said, 'which one should I have been?'

God forgive me, I accepted Resi as my Helga again.

Once she got that second acceptance, though, she began to show in little ways that her identification with Helga wasn't as complete as she'd said. She felt free, bit by bit, to accustom me to a personality that wasn't Helga's but her own.

This gradual revelation, this weaning of me from memories of Helga, began as we left the cafeteria. She asked me a jarringly practical question :

'Do you want me to keep on bleaching my hair white,' she said, 'or can I let it come back the way it really is?'

'What is it really?' I said.

'Honey,' she said.

'A lovely color for hair,' I said. 'Helga's color.'

'Mine has more red in it,' she said.

'I'd be interested to see it,' I said.

We walked up Fifth Avenue, and a little later she said to me, 'Will you write a play for me some time?'

'I don't know if I can write any more,' I said.

'Didn't Helga inspire you to write?' she said.

'Not to write, but to write the way I wrote,' I said.

'You wrote a special way – so she could play the part,' she said.

'That's right,' I said. 'I wrote parts for Helga that let her be the quintessence of Helga onstage.'

'I want you to do that for me some time,' she said.

'Maybe I'll try,' I said.

'The quintessence of Resi,' she said. 'Resi Noth.'

We saw a Veterans' Day parade down Fifth Avenue, and I heard Resi's laugh for the first time. It was nothing like Helga's laugh, which was a rustling thing. Resi's laugh was bright, melodious. What struck her so funny was the damn major-

89

ettes, kicking at the moon, twitching their behinds, and twirling chromium dildos.

'I've never seen such a thing before,' she said to me. 'War must be a very sexy thing to Americans.' She went on laughing and she thrust out her bosom to see if she might not make a good drum majorette, too.

She was growing younger by the second, gayer, more raucously irreverent. Her white hair, which had made me think so recently of premature aging, now updated itself, spoke of peroxide and girls who ran away to Hollywood.

When we turned away from the parade, we looked into a store window that showed a great gilded bed, one very much like the one Helga and I once had.

And not only did the window show that Wagnerian bed, it showed a reflection of Resi and me, too, ghostlike, and with a ghostly parade behind us. The pale wraiths and the substantial bed formed an unsettling composition. It seemed to be an allegory in the Victorian manner, a pretty good barroom painting, actually, with the passing banners and the golden bed and the male and female ghosts.

What the allegory was, I cannot say. But I can offer a few more clues. The male ghost looked God-awful old and starved and moth-eaten. The female ghost looked young enough to be his daughter, sleek, bouncy, and full of hell.

25 : The Answer to Communism . . .

Resi and I dawdled on our way back to my ratty attic, looked at furniture, drank here and there.

Resi went to the ladies' room in one bar, leaving me alone. A barfly started talking to me.

'You know what the answer to communism is?' he asked me.

'Nope,' I said.

'Moral Rearmament,' he said.

'What the hell is that?' I said.

'It's a movement,' he said.

'In what direction?' I said.

'That Moral Rearmament movement,' he said, 'believes in absolute honesty, absolute purity, absolute unselfishness, and absolute love.'

'I certainly wish them all the luck in the world,' I said.

In another bar, Resi and I met a man who claimed he could satisfy, thoroughly satisfy, seven women in a night, provided they were all different.

'I mean really different,' he said.

Oh, God – the lives people try to lead.

Oh, God – what a world they try to lead them in!

Resi and I didn't get home until after supper, after dark. Our
plan was to spend another night at a hotel. We came home because Resi wanted to have a waking dream of how we would
refurnish the attic, wanted to play house.

'At last I have a house,' she said.

'It takes a heap of living,' I said, 'to make a house a home.'
I saw that my mailbox was stuffed again. I left the mail where
it was.

'Who did that?' said Resi.

'Who did what?' I said.

'That,' she said, pointing to my namecard on the mailbox.
Somebody had drawn a swastika after my name in blue ink.

'It's something quite new,' I said uneasily. 'Maybe we'd better not go upstairs. Maybe whoever did it is up there.'

'I don't understand,' she said.

'You picked a miserable time to come to me, Resi,' I said.
'I had a cozy little burrow, where you and I might have been
quite content –'

'Burrow?' she said.

'A hole in the ground, made secret and snug,' I said. 'But,
God! –' I said in anguish, 'just when you were coming to me,
something laid my den wide open!' I told her how my notor-
iety had been renewed. 'Now the carnivores,' I said, 'scenting
a freshly opened den, are closing in.'

'Go to another country,' she said.

'What other country?' I said.

'Any country you like,' she said. 'You have the money to
go anywhere you want.'

'Anywhere I want –' I said.

And then a bald, bristly fat man carrying a shopping bag

came in. He shouldered Resi and me away from the mail-boxes with a hoarse, unapologetic bully's apology.

' 'Scuse me,' he said. He read the names on the mailboxes like a first-grader, putting a finger under each name, studying each name for a long, long time.

'Campbell!' he said at last, with massive satisfaction. 'Howard W. Campbell.' He turned to me accusingly. 'You know him?' he said.

'No,' I said.

'No,' he said, becoming radiant with malevolence. 'You look just like him.' He took a copy of the *Daily News* from the shopping bag, opened it to an inside page, handed it to Resi. 'Now, don't that look a lot like the gentleman you're with?' he said to her.

'Let me see,' I said. I took the paper from Resi's slack fingers, saw the picture of myself and Lieutenant O'Hare, standing before the gallows at Ohrdurf so long ago.

The story underneath the picture said that the government of Israel had located me after a fifteen-year search. That government was now requesting that the United States release me to Israel for trial. What did they want to try me for? Complicity in the murder of six million Jews.

The man hit me right through the newspaper before I could comment.

Down I went, banging my head on an ash can.

The man stood over me. 'Before the Jews put you in a cage in a zoo or whatever they're gonna do to you,' he said, 'I'd just like to play a little with you myself.'

I shook my head, trying to clear it.

'Felt that one, did you?' he said.

'Yes,' I said.

'That one was for Private Irving Buchanon,' he said.

'Is that who you are?' I said.

'Buchanon is dead,' he said. 'He was the best friend I ever had. Five miles in from Omaha Beach, the Germans cut his nuts off and hung him from a telephone pole.'

He kicked me in the ribs, holding Resi off with one hand. 'That's for Ansel Brewer,' he said, 'run over by a Tiger tank at Aachen.'

He kicked me again. 'That's for Eddie McCarty, cut in two by a burp gun in the Ardennes,' he said. 'Eddie was gonna be a doctor.'

He drew back his big foot to kick me in the head. 'And this one –' he said, and that's the last I heard. The kick was for somebody else who'd been killed in war. It knocked me cold.

Resi told me later what the last things the man said were, and what the present for me was in the shopping bag.

'I'm one guy who hasn't forgotten that war,' he said to me, though I could not hear him. 'Everybody else has forgot it, as near as I can tell – but not me.'

'I brought you this,' he said, 'so you could save everybody a lot of trouble.'

And he left.

Resi put the noose in the ash can, where it was found the next morning by a garbage-man named Lazlo Szombathy. Szombathy actually hanged himself with it – but that is another story.

As for my own story:

I regained consciousness on a ruptured studio couch in a damp, overheated room that was hung with mildewed Nazi banners. There was a cardboard fireplace, a dime-store's idea of how to have a merry Christmas. In it were cardboard birch logs, a red electric light and cellophane tongues of eternal fire.

Over this fireplace was a chromo of Adolf Hitler. It was swathed in black silk.

I myself was stripped to my olive-drab underwear, covered with a bedspread of simulated leopard skin. I groaned and sat up, skyrockets going off in my skull. I looked down at the leopard skin and mumbled something.

'What did you say, darling?' said Resi. She was sitting right beside the cot, though I hadn't seen her until she spoke.

'Don't tell me –' I said, drawing the leopard skin closer about me, 'I've joined the Hottentots.'

My research assistants here, lively, keen young people, have provided me with a photostat of a story in the New York *Times*, telling of the death of Lazlo Szombathy, the man who killed himself with the rope intended for me.

So I didn't dream that, either.

Szombathy did the big trick the night after I was beaten up.

He had come to this country after being a Freedom Fighter against the Russians in Hungary, according to the *Times*. He was a fratricide, according to the *Times*, having shot his brother Miklos, Second Minister of Education in Hungary.

Before he gave himself the big sleep, Szombathy wrote a note and pinned it to his trouser leg. There was nothing in the note about his having killed his brother.

His complaint was that he had been a respected veterinarian in Hungary, but that he was not permitted to practice in America. He had bitter things to say about freedom in America. He thought it was illusory.

In a final fandango of paranoia and masochism, Szombathy closed his note with a hint that he knew how to cure cancer. American doctors laughed at him, he said, whenever he tried to tell them how.

So much for Szombathy.

As for the room where I awakened after my beating: it was the cellar that had been furnished for the Iron Guard of the White Sons of the American Constitution by the late August Krapptauer, the cellar of Dr. Lionel J. D. Jones, D.D.S., D.D. Somewhere upstairs a printing press was running, turning out copies of *The White Christian Minuteman*.

From some other chamber in the cellar, partly sound-proofed, came the idiotically monotonous banging of target practice.

After my beating, I had been given first aid by young Dr.

Abraham Epstein, the doctor in my building who had pronounced Krapptauer dead. From Epstein's apartment, Resi had called Dr. Jones for help and advice.

'Why Jones?' I said.

'He was the only person in this country I knew I could trust,' said Resi. 'He was the only person I knew for sure was on your side.'

'What is life without friends?' I said.

I have no recollection of it, but Resi tells me that I regained consciousness in Epstein's apartment. Jones picked Resi and me up in his limousine, took me to a hospital, where I was X-rayed. I had three broken ribs taped up. After that I was taken to Jones' cellar and bedded down.

'Why here?' I said.

'It's safe,' said Resi.

'From what?' I said.

'The Jews,' she said.

The Black Fuehrer of Harlem, Jones' chauffeur, now came in with a tray of eggs, toast, and scalding coffee. He set it down on a table for me.

'Headache?' he asked me.

'Yes,' I said.

'Take an aspirin,' he said.

'Thank you for the advice,' I said.

'Most things in this world don't work —' he said, 'but aspirin do.'

'The — the Republic of Israel really wants me —' I said to Resi in groping disbelief, 'to — to try me for — for what the paper said?'

'Dr. Jones says the American Government won't let you go —' said Resi, 'but that the Jews will send men to kidnap you, the way they did Adolf Eichmann.'

'Such a piffling prisoner —' I murmured.

'Ain't like just having a Jew here and a Jew there after you,' said the Black Fuehrer.

'What?' I said.

'I mean,' he said, 'they got a country now. I mean, they got

Jewish battleships, they got Jewish airplanes, they got Jewish tanks. They got Jewish everything out after you but a Jewish hydrogen bomb.'

'Who in God's name is doing that shooting?' I said. 'Can't he stop until my head feels a little better?'

'That's your friend,' said Resi.

'Dr. Jones?' I said.

'George Kraft,' she said.

'Kraft?' I said. 'What's he doing here?'

'He's coming with us,' said Resi.

'To where?' I said.

'It's all been decided,' said Resi. 'Everybody agrees, darling – the best thing is for us to get out of the country. Dr. Jones has made arrangements.'

'What sort of arrangements?' I said.

'He has a friend with an airplane. As soon as you're well enough, darling, we get on the plane, fly to some divine place where you aren't known – and we'll start life all over again.'

I went to see George Kraft, there in Jones' basement. I found him standing at the head of a long corridor, the far end of which was packed with sandbags. Pinned to the sandbags was a target in the shape of a man.

The target was a caricature of a cigar-smoking Jew. The Jew was standing on broken crosses and little naked women. In one hand the Jew held a bag of money labeled 'International Banking.' In the other hand he held a Russian flag. From the pockets of his suit, little fathers, mothers, and children in scale with the naked women under his feet, cried out for mercy.

All these details were not evident from the far end of the shooting gallery, but it wasn't necessary for me to approach the target in order to know about them.

I had drawn the target in about 1941.

Millions of copies of the target were run off in Germany. It had so delighted my superiors that I was given a bonus of a ten-pound ham, thirty gallons of gasoline, and a week's all-expenses-paid vacation for my wife and myself at the *Schreiberhaus* in Riesengebirge.

I must admit that this target represents an excess of zeal, since I was not working as a graphic artist for the Nazis. I offer it in evidence against myself. I presume my authorship of it is news even to the Haifa Institute for the Documentation of War Criminals. I submit, however, that I drew the monster in order to establish myself even more solidly as a Nazi. I overdrew it, with an effect that would have been ludicrous anywhere but in Germany or Jones' basement, and I drew it far more amateurishly than I can really draw.

It succeeded, nonetheless.

I was flabbergasted by its success. The Hitler Youth and S.S. recruits fired at almost nothing else, and I even got a letter of thanks for the target from Heinrich Himmler.

'It has improved my marksmanship a hundred per cent,' he wrote. 'What pure Aryan can look at that wonderful target,' he said, 'and not shoot to kill?'

Watching Kraft pop away at that target, I understood its popularity for the first time. The amateurishness of it made it look like something drawn on the wall of a public lavatory; it recalled the stink, diseased twilight, humid resonance, and vile privacy of a stall in a public lavatory – echoed exactly the soul's condition in a man at war.

I had drawn better than I knew.

Kraft, oblivious to me in my leopard skin, fired again. He was using a Luger as big as a siege howitzer. It was chambered and bored for mere twenty-two's however, making anticlimactic, peewee *bangs*. Kraft fired again, and a sandbag two feet to the left of the target's head bled sand.

'Try opening your eyes the next time you fire,' I said.

'Oh –' he said, putting the pistol down, 'you're up and around.'

'Yes,' I said.

'Too bad what happened,' he said.

'I thought so,' I said.

'Maybe it's for the best, though,' he said. 'Maybe we'll all wind up thanking God it happened.'

'How so?' I said.

'It's jarred us out of our ruts,' he said.

'That's for certain,' I said.

'When you get out of this country with your girl, get yourself new surroundings, a new identity – you'll start writing again,' he said, 'and you'll write ten times better than you ever did before. Think of the maturity you'll be bringing to your writing!'

'My head aches too much just now –' I said.

'It'll stop aching soon,' he said. 'It isn't broken and it's filled with a heartbreakingly clear understanding of the self and the world.'

'Um,' I said.

'And I'm going to be a better painter for the change, too,'

he said. 'I've never seen the tropics before — that brutal glut of color, that visible, audible heat —'

'What's this about the tropics?' I said.

'I thought that's where we'd go,' he said. 'That's where Resi wants to go, too.'

'You're coming, too?' I said.

'Do you mind?' he said.

'People have certainly been active while I slept,' I said.

'Was that wrong of us?' said Kraft. 'Did we plan anything that would be bad for you?'

'George —' I said, 'why should you throw in your lot with us? Why should you come down into this cellar with the black beetles, too? You have no enemies. Stay with us, George, and you'll deserve every enemy I have.'

He put his hand on my shoulder, looked deep into my eyes. 'Howard —' he said, 'when my wife died, I had no allegiance to anything on earth. I, too, was a meaningless fragment of a nation of two.

'And then I discovered something I had never known before — what a true friend was,' he said. 'I throw my lot in with you gladly, friend. Nothing else interests me. Nothing else attracts me in the least. With your permission, my paints and I would like nothing better than to go with you wherever Fate takes you next.'

'This — this is friendship indeed,' I said.

'I hope so,' he said.

I spent two days in that queer basement – as a meditative invalid.

My clothes had been ruined in the beating I'd taken. So, from the resources of Jones' household, I was given other clothes. I was given a pair of shiny black trousers by Father Keeley, a silver-colored shirt by Dr. Jones, a shirt that had once been part of the uniform of a defunct American Fascist movement called, straightforwardly enough, 'The Silver Shirts.' And the Black Fuehrer gave me a tiny orange sports coat that made me look like an organ-grinder's monkey.

And Resi Noth and George Kraft kept me company tenderly – not only nursed me, but did my dreaming and planning for me as well. The big dream was to get out of America as soon as possible. Conversations, in which I took very little part, were a sort of roulette played with the names of warm places purported to be Edens: Acapulco ... Minorca ... Rhodes ... even the Vale of Kashmir, Zanzibar, and the Andaman Islands.

The news from the outside world was not such as to make my remaining in America attractive – or even conceivable. Father Keeley went out and bought newspapers several times a day, and, for supplementary enlightenment, we had the blatting of the radio.

The Republic of Israel stepped up its demands for me, encouraged by rumours that I wasn't an American citizen, that I was, in fact, a citizen of nowhere. And the Republic's demands were framed so as to be educational, too – teaching that a propagandist of my sort was as much a murderer as Heydrich, Eichmann, Himmler, or any of the gruesome rest.

That may be so. I had hoped, as a broadcaster, to be merely ludicrous, but this is a hard world to be ludicrous in, with so many human beings so reluctant to laugh, so incapable of thought, so eager to believe and snarl and hate. So many people *wanted* to believe me!

Say what you will about the sweet miracle of unquestioning faith, I consider a capacity for it terrifying and absolutely vile.

West Germany asked the Government of the United States politely if I might be a citizen of theirs. They had no proof one way or another, since all records pertaining to me had burned during the war. If I was a citizen of theirs, they said, they would be as pleased as Israel to have me for trial.

If I was a German, they said in effect, they were certainly ashamed of a German like me.

Soviet Russia, in short words that sounded like ball bearings being dropped into wet gravel, said that no trial was necessary. A Fascist like me, they said, should be squashed underfoot like a cockroach.

But it was the anger of my neighbors that really stank of sudden death. The more barbaric newspapers printed without comment letters from people who wanted me displayed from coast to coast in an iron cage; from heroes who volunteered to serve in a firing squad for me, as though the use of small arms were a skill known to few; from people who planned to do nothing themselves, but were confident enough in American civilization to know that there were other, stronger, younger people who would know what to do.

And these last-named patriots were right in having confidence. I doubt if there has ever been a society that has been without strong and young people eager to experiment with homicide, provided no very awful penalties are attached to it.

According to the newspapers and radio, justifiably angry people had already done what they could about me, breaking into my ratty attic, smashing my windows, tearing up or carting off my worldly goods. The hated attic was now under police guard around the clock.

The New York *Post* pointed out editorially that the police could scarcely give me the protection I needed, since my enemies were so numerous and so understandably murderous. What was called for, said the *Post* helplessly, was a battalion of Marines to surround me for the rest of my days.

The New York *Daily News* suggested that my biggest war crime was not killing myself like a gentleman. Presumably Hitler was a gentleman.

The *News*, incidentally, also printed a letter from Bernard B. O'Hare, the man who had captured me in Germany, the man who had recently written me a letter with copious carbons.

'I want this guy all for myself,' O'Hare wrote me. 'I deserve this guy all for myself. I was the guy who caught him in Germany. If I'd known then he was going to get away, I would have blown his head off right then and there. If anybody sees Campbell before I do, tell him Bernie O'Hare is on his way from Boston by nonstop plane.'

The New York *Times* said that tolerating and even protecting vermin like me was one of the maddening necessities in the life of a truly free society.

The United States Government, as Resi had told me, was not going to turn me over to the Republic of Israel. There was no legal machinery for that.

The United States Government did promise, however, to make a full and open review of my puzzling case, to find out exactly what my citizenship status was, to find out why I had never even been brought to trial.

That Government expressed queasy surprise that I was even within its borders.

The New York *Times* published a portrait of me as a much younger man, my official portrait as a Nazi and idol of the international airwaves. I can only guess at the year in which the picture was taken – 1941, I think.

Arndt Klopfer, the photographer who took the picture of me, did his best to make me look like a Maxfield Parrish Jesus covered with cold cream. He even gave me a halo, a judiciously placed spot of nebulous light in the background.

The halo was no special effect for me alone. Everybody who went to Klopfer got a halo, including Adolf Eichmann.

I can say that for certain about Eichmann, without asking for confirmation from the Haifa Institute, because Eichmann had his picture taken just ahead of me at Klopfer's studio. It was the only time I ever met Eichmann – the only time in Germany. I met him again here in Israel – only two weeks ago, when I was incarcerated briefly in Tel Aviv.

About that reunion: I was locked up in Tel Aviv for twenty-four hours. On my way to my cell there, the guards stopped me outside Eichmann's cell to hear what we had to say to each other, if anything.

We didn't recognize each other, and the guards had to introduce us.

Eichmann was writing the story of his life, just as I am now writing the story of my life. That chinless old plucked buzzard, with six million murders to explain away, gave me a saintly smile. He was sweetly interested in his work, in me, in the guards in the prison, in everybody.

He beamed at me, and he said, 'I'm not mad at anybody.'

'That's certainly the way to be,' I said.

'I've got some advice for you,' he said.

'I'd be glad to have it,' I said.

'Relax,' he said, beaming, beaming, beaming. 'Just relax.'

'That's how I got here,' I said.

'Life is divided up into phases,' he said. 'Each one is very different from the others, and you have to be able to recognize what is expected of you in each phase. That's the secret of successful living.'

'It's good of you to share the secret with me,' I said.

'I'm a writer now,' he said. 'I never thought I'd be a writer.'

'May I ask a personal question?' I said.

'Certainly,' he said benignly. 'That's the phase I'm in now. This is the time for thinking and answering. Ask whatever you like.'

'Do you feel that you're guilty of murdering six million Jews?' I said.

'Absolutely not,' said the architect of Auschwitz, the introducer of conveyor belts into crematoria, the greatest customer in the world for the gas called Cyklon-B.

Not knowing the man for sure, I tried some intramural satire on him – what seemed to me to be intramural satire. 'You were simply a soldier, were you –' I said, 'taking orders from higher-ups, like soldiers around the world?'

Eichmann turned to a guard, and talked to him in rapid-fire Yiddish, indignant Yiddish. If he'd spoken it slowly, I would have understood it, but he spoke too fast.

'What did he say?' I asked the guard.

'He wondered if we'd showed you his statement,' said the guard. 'He made us promise not to show it to anybody until it was done.'

'I haven't seen it,' I said to Eichmann.

'Then how do you know what my defense is going to be?' he said.

This man actually believed that he had invented his own trite defense, though a whole nation of ninety some-odd million had made the same defense before him. Such was his paltry understanding of the God-like human act of invention.

The more I think about Eichmann and me, the more I think that he should be sent to the hospital, and that I am the sort of person for whom punishments by fair, just men were devised.

As a friend of the court that will try Eichmann, I offer my opinion that Eichmann cannot distinguish between right and wrong – that not only right and wrong, but truth and falsehood, hope and despair, beauty and ugliness, kindness and cruelty, comedy and tragedy, are all processed by Eichmann's mind indiscriminately, like birdshot through a bugle.

My case is different. I always know when I tell a lie, am capable of imagining the cruel consequences of anybody's believing my lies, know cruelty is wrong. I could no more lie without noticing it than I could unknowingly pass a kidney stone.

If there is another life after this one, I would like very much, in the next one, to be the sort of person of whom it could truly be said, 'Forgive him – he knows not what he does.'

This cannot be said of me now.

The only advantage to me of knowing the difference between right and wrong, as nearly as I can tell, is that I can sometimes laugh when the Eichmanns can see nothing funny.

'You still write?' Eichmann asked me, there in Tel Aviv.

'One last project –' I said, 'a command performance for the archives.'

'You are a professional writer?' he said.

'Some say so,' I said.

'Tell me –' he said, 'do you set a certain time of day aside for writing, whether you feel like it or not – or do you wait for inspiration to strike, night or day?'

'A schedule,' I said, remembering back so many years.

I got some of his respect back. 'Yes, yes –' he said, nodding, 'a schedule. That's what I've found, too. Sometimes I simply stare at a blank sheet of paper, but I still sit here and stare at it for the whole period I've set aside for work. Does alcohol help?'

'I think it only seems to – and only seems to for about half an hour,' I said. This, too, was an opinion from my youth.

Eichmann made a joke. 'Listen –' he said, 'about those six million –'

'Yes?' I said.

'I could spare you a few for your book,' he said. 'I don't think I really need them all.'

I offer this joke to history, on the assumption that no tape recorder was around. This was one of the memorable quips of the bureaucratic Genghis Khan.

It's possible that Eichmann wanted me to recognize that I had killed a lot of people, too, by the exercise of my fat mouth. But I doubt that he was that subtle a man, man of as many parts as he was. I think, if we ever got right down to it, that, out of the six million murders generally regarded as his, he wouldn't lend me so much as one. If he were to start farming out all those murders, after all, Eichmann as Eichmann's idea of Eichmann would disappear.

The guards took me away, and the only other encounter I had with the Man of the Century was in the form of a note, smuggled mysteriously from his prison in Tel Aviv to mine in Jerusalem. The note was dropped at my feet by a person unknown in the exercise yard here. I picked it up, read it, and this is what it said:

'Do you think a literary agent is absolutely necessary?' The note was signed by Eichmann.

My reply was this: 'For book club and movie sales in the United States of America, absolutely.'

We would fly to Mexico City – Kraft, Resi, and I. That became the plan. Dr. Jones would not only provide us with transportation, he would provide us with a reception committee in Mexico City as well.

From Mexico City we would go exploring by automobile, would seek some secret village in which to spend the rest of our days.

The plan was surely as charming a daydream as I had had in many a day. And it seemed not only possible but certain that I would write again.

Shyly, I told Resi so.

She wept for joy. For real joy? Who knows. I can only guarantee that the tears were wet and salty.

'Did I have anything to do with this lovely, this heavenly miracle?' she said.

'Everything,' I said, holding her close.

'No, no – very little –' she said, 'but some – thank God, some. The big miracle is the talent you were born with.'

'The big miracle,' I said, 'is your power to raise the dead.'

'Love does that,' she said. 'And it raised me, too. How alive do you think I was – before?'

'Shall I write about it?' I said. 'In our village there in Mexico, on the rim of the Pacific – is that what I should write first?'

'Yes – yes, oh yes – darling, darling,' she said. 'I'll take such good care of you while you do it. Will – will you have any time for me?'

'The afternoons and the evenings and the nights,' I said. 'That's all the time I'll be able to give you.'

'Have you decided on a name yet?' she said.

'Name?' I said.

'Your new name – the name of the new writer whose beautiful works come mysteriously out of Mexico,' she said. 'I will be Mrs. —'

'*Señora* —' I said.

'Señora who?' she said. 'Señor and Señora who?'

'Christen us,' I said.

'It's too important for me to decide right away,' she said.

Kraft came in at this point.

Resi asked him to suggest a pseudonym for me.

'What about Don Quixote?' he said. 'That,' he said to Resi, 'would make you Dulcinea del Toboso, and I would sign my paintings Sancho Panza.'

Dr. Jones now came in with Father Keeley. 'The plane will be ready tomorrow morning,' he said. 'You're sure you'll be well enough to travel?'

'I'm well enough right now,' I said.

'The man who'll meet you in Mexico City is Arndt Klopfer,' said Jones. 'Can you remember that?'

'The photographer?' I said.

'You know him?' said Jones.

'He took my official photograph in Berlin,' I said.

'He's the biggest brewer in Mexico now,' said Jones.

'For God's sake,' I said. 'The last I heard, his studio got hit with a five-hundred-pound bomb.'

'You can't keep a good man down,' said Jones. 'Now then — Father Keeley and I have a special request to make of you.'

'Oh?' I said.

'Tonight is the weekly meeting of the Iron Guard of the White Sons of the Constitution,' said Jones. 'Father Keeley and I want to stage some sort of memorial service for August Krapptauer.'

'I see,' I said.

'Father Keeley and I don't think we could deliver the eulogy without breaking down,' said Jones. 'It would be a terrible emotional ordeal for either one of us. We wonder if you, a very famous speaker, a man with a golden tongue, if I may say so — we were wondering if you would accept the honor of saying a few words.'

I could hardly refuse. 'Thank you, gentlemen,' I said. 'A eulogy?'

'Father Keeley thought up a general theme, if that would help,' said Jones.

'It would help a lot, a general theme would,' I said. 'I could certainly use one.'

Father Keeley cleared his throat. 'I think the theme should be,' that addled old cleric said, 'His Truth Goes Marching On.'

The Iron Guard of the White Sons of the American Constitution assembled on ranks of folding chairs in the furnace room of Dr. Jones' basement. The guardsmen were twenty in number, ranging in age from sixteen to twenty. They were all blond. They were all over six feet tall.

They were neatly dressed, wore suits and white shirts and neckties. All that identified them as guardsmen was a little piece of gold ribbon run through the buttonhole of the right lapel of each.

I would not have noticed this odd detail of buttonholes on the right lapels, that conventionally have no buttonholes, if Dr. Jones hadn't pointed it out to me.

'It's a way they have of identifying each other, even though the ribbon isn't worn,' he said. 'They can see their ranks growing,' he said, 'without anybody else noticing it.'

'They all have to take their coats to tailors and insist on buttonholes in the right lapel?' I said.

'The mothers do it,' said Father Keeley.

Keeley, Jones, Resi, and I were sitting on a raised platform facing the guardsmen, our backs to the furnace. Resi was on the platform because she had agreed to say a few words to the boys about her firsthand experiences with communism behind the Iron Curtain.

'Most tailors are Jews,' said Dr. Jones. 'We don't want to tip our hand.'

'Besides —' said Father Keeley, 'it's good for the mothers to participate.'

Jones' chauffeur, The Black Fuehrer of Harlem, was now on the platform with us, hanging a big canvas sign behind us, tying its grommeted ends to steam pipes.

This is what it said:

'Get plenty of education. Lead your class in all things. Keep your body clean and strong. Keep your opinions to yourself.'

'These are neighborhood kids?' I asked Jones.

'Oh, no,' said Jones. 'Only eight of them are even from New York City. Nine are from New Jersey, two are from Peekskill – the twins – and one comes all the way from Philadelphia.'

'Every week he comes from Philadelphia?' I said.

'Where else can he get what August Krapptauer was offering here?' said Jones.

'How were they recruited?' I said.

'Through my paper,' said Jones, 'but they really recruited themselves. Worried, conscientious parents were writing to *The White Christian Minuteman* all the time, asking me if there wasn't some youth movement that wanted to keep the American bloodstream pure. One of the most heartbreaking letters I ever saw was from a woman in Bernardsville, New Jersey. She'd let her boy go into the Boy Scouts of America, not knowing that the true name of the B.S.A. ought to be "the Boogies and Semites of America." And the boy got to be an Eagle Scout, and then he went into the Army, went over to Japan, and came home with a Japanese wife.'

'When August Krapptauer read that letter he cried,' said Father Keeley. 'That's when he knew, tired as he was, he had to get back to working with youth again.'

Father Keeley called the meeting to order, had us all pray. His prayer was a conventional one, asking for courage in the face of hostile hosts.

There was one unconventional touch, however, a touch I had never heard of before, even in Germany. The Black Fuehrer stood over a kettledrum in the back of the room. The drum was muffled – muffled, as it happened, by the simulated leopard skin I had worn earlier for a bathrobe. At the end of each sentence in the prayer, the Black Fuehrer gave the muffled drum a thump.

Resi's talk on the horrors of life behind the Iron Curtain was brief and dull, and so unsatisfactory from an educational standpoint that Jones had to prompt her.

'Most devoted Communists are of Jewish or Oriental blood, aren't they?' he asked her.

'What?' she said.

'Of course they are,' said Jones. 'It goes without saying,' he said, and he dismissed her rather curtly.

Where was George Kraft? He was sitting in the audience, in the very last row, next to the muffled kettledrum.

Jones introduced me next, introduced me as a man who needed no introduction. He said I wasn't to start talking yet, because he had a surprise for me.

He certainly did.

The Black Fuehrer left his drum, went to a rheostat by the light switch, and dimmed the lights gradually as Jones talked.

Jones told, in the gathering darkness, of the intellectual and moral climate in America during the Second World War. He told of how patriotic, thoughtful white men were persecuted for their ideals, how, finally, almost all the American patriots were rotting in federal dungeons.

'Nowhere could an American find the truth,' he said.

The room was pitch dark now.

'Almost nowhere,' said Jones in the dark. 'If a man was fortunate enough to have a short-wave radio,' he said, 'there was still one fountainhead of truth – just one.'

And then, in the darkness, there was the crackle and susurrus of short-wave static, a fragment of French, a fragment of German, a fragment of Brahms' First Symphony, as though played on a Kazoos – and then, loud and clear –

This is Howard W. Campbell, Jr., one of the few remaining free Americans, speaking to you from free Berlin. I wish to welcome my countrymen, which is to say the native white gentiles, of the 106th Division, taking up positions before St. Vith tonight. To the parents of the boys in this green division, may I say that the area is presently a quiet one. The 442nd and 444th Regiments are one line – the 423rd in reserve.

There is a fine article in the current *Reader's Digest*

with the title, 'There are No Atheists in Foxholes.' I should like to expand this theme a little and tell you that, even though this is a war inspired by the Jews, a war that only the Jews can win, there are no Jews in foxholes, either. The riflemen in the 106th can tell you that. The Jews are all too busy counting merchandise in the Quartermaster Corps or money in the Finance Corps or selling black-market cigarettes and nylons in Paris to ever come closer to the front than a hundred miles.

You folks at home, you parents and relatives of boys at the front – I want you to think of all the Jews you know. I want you to think hard about them.

Now then – let me ask you, is the war making them richer or poorer? Do they eat better or worse than you under supposed rationing? Do they dress better or worse than you do? Do they seem to have more or less gasoline than you do?

I already know what the answers to all those questions are, and so will you, if you'll open your eyes and think hard for a minute.

Now let me ask you this:

Do you know of a single Jewish family that has received a telegram from Washington, once the capital of a free people – do you know of a single Jewish family that has received a telegram from Washington that begins, 'The Secretary of War desires me to express his deep regret that your son . . .'

And so on.

There were fifteen minutes of Howard W. Campbell, Jr., the free American, there in basement darkness. I do not mean to suppress my infamy with a casual 'and so on.'

The Haifa Institute for the Documentation of War Criminals has recordings of every broadcast Howard W. Campbell, Jr., ever made. If someone wants to go over those broadcasts, wants to cull from them the very worst things I said, I have no objection to those culls being attached to this account as an appendix.

I can hardly deny that I said them. All I can say is that I didn't believe them, that I knew full well what ignorant, destructive, obscenely jocular things I was saying.

The experience of sitting there in the dark, hearing the things I'd said, didn't shock me. It might be helpful in my defense to say that I broke into a cold sweat, or some such nonsense. But I've always known what I did. I've always been able to live with what I did. How? Through that simple and widespread boon to modern mankind – schizophrenia.

There was one adventure in the dark worth reporting, though. Somebody put a note in my pocket, did it with intentional clumsiness, so that I would know the note was there.

When the light came on again, I could not guess who had given me the note.

I delivered my eulogy of August Krapptauer, saying, incidentally, what I pretty much believe, that Krapptauer's sort of truth would probably be with mankind forever, as long as there were men and women around who listened to their hearts instead of their minds.

I got a nice round of applause from the audience, and a drum-roll from the Black Fuehrer.

I went into the lavatory to read the note.

The note was printed on lined paper torn from a small spiral notebook. This is what it said:

'Coal-bin door unlocked. Leave at once. I am waiting for you in vacant store directly across street. Urgent. Your life in danger. Eat this.'

It was signed by my Blue Fairy Godmother, by Colonel Frank Wirtanen.

32: Rosenfeld . . .

My lawyer here in Jerusalem, Mr. Alvin Dobrowitz, has told me that I would surely win my case if I could produce one witness who had seen me in the company of the man known to me as Colonel Frank Wirtanen.

I met Wirtanen three times: before the war, immediately after the war, and finally, in the back of a vacant store across the street from the residence of The Reverend Doctor Lionel J. D. Jones, D.D.S., D.D. Only at the first meeting, the meeting on the park bench, did anyone see us together. And those who saw us were no more likely to fix us in their memories than were the squirrels and birds.

The second time I met him was in Wiesbaden, Germany, in the dining hall of what had once been an officers' candidate school of the Engineers Corps of the *Wehrmacht*. There was a great mural on the wall of that dining hall, a tank coming down a lovely, winding country lane. The sun was shining in the mural. The sky was clear. This bucolic scene was about to be shattered.

In a thicket, in the foreground of the mural, was a merry little band of steel-helmeted Robin Hoods, engineers whose latest prank was to mine the lane and to implement the impending merriment with an anti-tank gun and a light machine gun.

They were so happy.

How did I get to Wiesbaden?

I was taken from a Third Army prisoner-of-war pen near Ohrdruf on April 15, three days after my capture by Lieutenant Bernard B. O'Hare.

I was driven to Wiesbaden in a jeep, was guarded by a first lieutenant whose name is unknown to me. We didn't talk much. I did not interest him. He spent the entire trip in a slow-smoldering rage about something that had nothing to do with

117

me.. Had he been slighted, insulted, cheated, maligned, grievously misunderstood? I don't know.

At any rate, I don't think he would be much help as a witness. He was carrying out orders that bored him. He asked his way to the camp, and then to the dining hall. He left me at the door of the dining hall, told me to go inside and wait. And then he drove off, leaving me unguarded.

I went inside, though I might easily have wandered into the countryside again.

Inside that melancholy barn, all alone, seated on a table under the mural, was my Blue Fairy Godmother.

Wirtanen was wearing the uniform of an American soldier – zippered jacket; olive-drab trousers and shirt, the shirt open at the neck; combat boots. He had no weapon. Neither did he wear any symbol of rank or unit.

He was a short-legged man. When I saw him sitting there on the table, he was swinging his feet, and his feet were far off the floor. He must have been at least fifty-five then, seven years older than when last I'd seen him. He was bald, had put on weight.

Colonel Frank Wirtanen had the impudent, pink-baby look that victory and an American combat uniform seemed to produce in so many older men.

He beamed at me and he shook my hand warmly, and he said, 'Well – what did you think of *that* war, Campbell?'

'I would just as soon have stayed out of it,' I said.

'Congratulations,' he said. 'You lived through it, anyway. A lot of people didn't, you know.'

'I know,' I said. 'My wife, for instance.'

'Sorry about that,' he said.

'I found out she was missing the same day you did,' he said.

'How?' I said.

'From you,' he said. 'That was one of the pieces of information you broadcast that night.'

This news, that I had broadcast the coded announcement of my Helga's disappearance, broadcast it without even knowing what I was doing, somehow upset me more than anything in the whole adventure. It upsets me even now. Why, I don't know.

It represented, I suppose, a wider separation of my several selves than even I can bear to think about.

At that climactic moment in my life, when I had to suppose that my Helga was dead, I would have liked to mourn as an agonized soul, indivisible. But no. One part of me told the world of the tragedy in code. The rest of me did not even know that the announcement was being made.

'That was vital military information? That had to be got out of Germany at the risk of my neck?' I said to Wirtanen.

'Certainly,' he said. 'The instant we got it, we began to act.'

'To act?' I said, mystified. 'To act how?'

'To find a replacement for you,' said Wirtanen. 'We thought you'd kill yourself before the sun came up again.'

'I should have,' I said.

'I'm damn glad you didn't,' he said.

'I'm damn sorry I didn't,' I said. 'You would think that a man who's spent as much time in the theater as I have would know when the proper time came for the hero to die – if he was to be a hero.' I snapped my fingers softly. 'There goes the whole play about Helga and me, "Nation of Two," ' I said, 'because I missed my cue for the great suicide scene.'

'I don't admire suicide,' said Wirtanen.

'I admire form,' I said. 'I admire things with a beginning, a middle, an end – and, whenever possible, a moral, too.'

'There's a chance she's still alive, I guess,' said Wirtanen.

'A loose end,' I said. 'An irrelevancy. The play is over.'

'You said something about a moral?' he said.

'If I'd killed myself when you expected me to kill myself,' I said, 'maybe a moral would have occurred to you.'

'I'll have to think –' he said.

'Take your time,' I said.

'I'm not used to things having form – or morals, either,' he said. 'If you'd died, I probably would have said something like, "Goddamn, now what'll we do?" A moral? It's a big enough job just burying the dead, without trying to draw a moral from each death,' he said. 'Half the dead don't even have names. I might have said you were a good soldier.'

'Was I?' I said.

'Of all the agents who were my dream children, so to speak, you were the only one who got clear through the war both reliable and alive,' he said. 'I did a little morbid arithmetic last night, Campbell – calculated that you, by being neither incompetent nor dead, were one in 'forty-two.'

'What about the people who fed me information?' I said.

'Dead, all dead,' he said. 'Every one of them a woman, by the way. Seven of them, in all – each one of them, before she was caught, living only to transmit information to you. Think of it Campbell – seven women you satisfied again and again and again – and they finally died for the satisfaction that was yours to give them. And not one of them betrayed you, either, when she was caught. Think of that, too.'

'I can't say you've relieved any shortage of things to think about,' I said to Wirtanen. 'I don't mean to diminish your stature as a teacher and philosopher, but I had things to think about even before this happy reunion. So what happens to me next?'

'You've already disappeared again,' he said. 'Third Army's been relieved of you, and there'll be no records here to show that you ever arrived.' He spread his hands. 'Where would you like to go from here, and who would you like to be?'

'I don't suppose there's a hero's welcome awaiting me anywhere,' I said.

'Hardly,' he said.

'Any news of my parents?' I said.

'I'm sorry to tell you –' he said, 'they died four months ago.'

'Both?' I said.

'Your father first – your mother twenty-four hours later. Heart both times,' he said.

I cried a little about that, shook my head. 'Nobody told them what I was really doing?' I said.

'Our radio station in the heart of Berlin was worth more than the peace of mind of two old people,' he said.

'I wonder,' I said.

'You're entitled to wonder,' he said. 'I'm not.'

'How many people knew what I was doing?' I said.

'The good things or the bad things?' he said.

'The good,' I said.

'Three of us,' he said.

'That's all?' I said.

'That's a lot,' he said. 'Too many, really. There was me, there was General Donovan, and one other.'

'Three people in all the world knew me for what I was –' I said. 'And all the rest –' I shrugged.

'They knew you for what you were, too,' he said abruptly.

'That wasn't me,' I said, startled by his sharpness.

'Whoever it was –' said Wirtanen, 'he was one of the most vicious sons of bitches who ever lived.'

I was amazed. Wirtanen was sincerely bitter.

'You give me hell for that – knowing what you do?' I said. 'How else could I have survived?'

'That was your problem,' he said. 'Very few men could have solved it as thoroughly as you did.'

'You think I was a Nazi?' I said.

'Certainly you were,' he said. 'How else could a responsible historian classify you? Let me ask you a question –'

'Ask away,' I said.

'If Germany had won, had conquered the world –' he stopped, cocked his head. 'You must be way ahead of me. You must know what the question is.'

'How would I have lived?' I said. 'What would I have felt? What would I have done?'

'Exactly,' he said. 'You must have thought about it, with an imagination like yours.'

'My imagination isn't what it used to be,' I said. 'One of the first things I discovered when I became an agent was that I couldn't afford an imagination any more.'

'No answer to my question?' he said.

'Now is as good a time as any to see if I've got any imagination left,' I said. 'Give me a minute or two –'

'Take all the time you want,' he said.

So I projected myself into the situation he described, and what was left of my imagination gave me a corrosively cynical answer. 'There is every chance,' I said, 'that I would have become a sort of Nazi Edgar Guest, writing a daily column of optimistic doggerel for daily papers around the world. And, as senility set in – the sunset of life, as they say – I might even come to believe what my couplets said: that everything was probably all for the best.'

I shrugged. 'Would I have shot anybody? I doubt it. Would I have organized a bomb plot? That's more of a possibility; but I've heard a lot of bombs go off in my time, and they never impressed me much as a way to get things done. Only one thing can I guarantee you: I would never have written a play again. That skill, such as it was, is lost.

'The only chance of my doing something really violent in favor of truth or justice or what have you,' I said to my Blue Fairy Godmother, 'would lie in my going homicidally insane. That could happen. In the situation you suggest, I might suddenly run amok with a deadly weapon down a peaceful street on an ordinary day. But whether the killing I did would improve the world much would be a matter of dumb luck, pure and simple.

'Have I answered your question honestly enough for you?' I asked him.

'Yes, thank you,' he said.

'Classify me as a Nazi,' I said tiredly. 'Classify away. Hang me, if you think it would tend to raise the general level of morality. This life is no great treasure. I have no postwar plans.'

'I only want you to understand how little we can do for you,' he said. 'I see you do understand.'

'How little?' I said.

'A false identity, a few red herrings, transportation to

wherever you might conceivably start a new life –' he said. 'Some cash. Not much, but some.'

'Cash?' I said. 'How was the cash value of my services arrived at?'

'A matter of custom,' he said, 'a custom going back to at least the Civil War.'

'Oh?' I said.

'Private's pay,' he said. 'On my say-so, you're entitled to it for the period from when we met in the Tiergarten to the present.'

'That's very generous,' I said.

'Generosity doesn't amount to much in this business,' he said. 'The really good agents aren't interested in money at all. Would it make any difference to you if we gave you the back pay of a brigadier general?'

'No,' I said.

'Or if we paid you nothing at all?'

'No difference,' I said.

'It's almost never money,' he said. 'Or patriotism, either.'

'What is it, then?' I said.

'Each person has to answer that question for himself –' said Wirtanen. 'Generally speaking, espionage offers each spy an opportunity to go crazy in a way he finds irresistible.'

'Interesting,' I said emptily.

He clapped his hands to break the mood. 'Now then –' he said, 'about transportation: where to?'

'Tahiti?' I said.

'If you say so,' he said. 'I suggest New York. You can lose yourself there without any trouble, and there's plenty of work, if you want it.'

'All right – New York,' I said.

'Let's get your passport picture taken. You'll be on a plane out of here inside of three hours,' he said.

We crossed the deserted parade ground together, dust devils spinning here and there. It was my fancy to think of the dust devils as the spooks of former cadets at the school, killed in war, returning now to whirl and dance on the parade ground alone, to dance in as unmilitary a fashion as they damn well pleased.

'When I told you there were only three people who knew about your coded broadcasts –' said Wirtanen.

'What about it?' I said.

'You didn't ask who the third one was,' he said.

'Would it be anybody I'd ever heard of?' I said.

'Yes,' he said. 'He's dead now, I'm sorry to say. You used to attack him regularly in your broadcasts.'

'Oh?' I said.

'The man you called Franklin Delano Rosenfeld,' said Wirtanen. 'He used to listen to you gleefully every night.'

The third time I met my Blue Fairy Godmother, and the last time, from all indications, was, as I have said, in a vacant shop across the street from the house of Jones, across the street from where Resi, George Kraft and I were hiding.

I took my time about going into that dark place, expecting, with reason, to find anything from an American Legion color guard to a platoon of Israeli paratroopers waiting to capture me inside.

I had a pistol with me, one of the Iron Guard's Lugers, chambered for twenty-two's. I had it not in my pocket but in the open, loaded and cocked, ready to go. I scouted the front of the shop without showing myself. The front was dark. And then I approached the back in short rushes, from cluster to cluster of garbage cans.

Anybody trying to jump me, to jump Howard W. Campbell, Jr., would have been filled with little holes, as though by a sewing machine. And I must say that I came to love the infantry, anybody's infantry, in that series of rushes and taking cover.

Man, I think, is an infantry animal.

There was a light in the back of the shop. I looked through a window and saw a scene of great serenity. Colonel Frank Wirtanen, my Blue Fairy Godmother, was sitting on a table again, waiting for me again.

He was an old, old man now, as sleek and hairless as Buddha. I went in.

'I thought surely you would have retired by now,' I said.

'I did –' he said, 'eight years ago. Built a house on a lake in Maine with an axe and an adze and my own two hands. I was called out of retirement as a specialist.'

'In what?' I said.

'In you,' he said.

'Why the sudden interest in me?' I said.

'That's what I'm supposed to find out,' he said.

'No mystery why the Israelis would want me,' I said.

'I agree,' he said. 'But there's a lot of mystery about why the Russians should think you were such a fat prize.'

'Russians?' I said. 'What Russians?'

'The girl, Resi Noth – and the old man, the painter, the one called George Kraft,' said Wirtanen. 'They're both communist agents. We've been watching the one who calls himself Kraft now since 1941. We made it easy for the girl to get into the country just to find out what she hoped to do.'

I sat wretchedly on a packing case. 'With a few well-chosen words,' I said, 'you've wiped me out. How much poorer I am in this minute than I was in the minute before!

'Friend, dream, and mistress –' I said, '*alles kaput.*'

'You've still got the friend,' said Wirtanen.

'What do you mean by that?' I said.

'He's like you,' said Wirtanen. 'He can be many things at once – all sincerely.' He smiled. 'It's a gift.'

'What was he planning for me?' I said.

'He wanted to uproot you from this country, get you to another one, where you could be kidnapped with fewer international complications. He tipped off Jones as to where and who you were, got O'Hare and other patriots all stirred up about you again – all as part of a scheme to pull up your roots.'

'Mexico – that was the dream he gave me,' I said.

'I know,' said Wirtanen. 'There's a plane waiting for you in Mexico City right now. If you were to fly down there, you wouldn't spend more than two minutes on the ground. Off you'd go again, bound for Moscow in the latest jet, all expenses paid.'

'Dr. Jones is in on this, too?' I said.

'No,' said Wirtanen. 'He's got your best interests at heart. He's one of the few men you can trust.'

'Why should they want me in Moscow?' I said. 'What do the Russians want with me – with such a moldy old piece of surplus from World War Two?'

'They want to exhibit you to the world as a prime example of the sort of Fascist war criminal this country shelters,' said Wirtanen. 'They also hope that you will confess to all sorts of collusion between Americans and Nazis at the start of the Nazi regime.'

'Why would I confess such a thing?' I said. 'What did they plan to threaten me with?'

'That's simple,' said Wirtanen. 'That's obvious.'

'Torture?' I said.

'Probably not,' said Wirtanen. 'Just death.'

'I don't fear it,' I said.

'Oh, it wouldn't be for you,' said Wirtanen.

'For whom, then?' I said.

'For the girl you love, for the girl who loves you —' said Wirtanen. 'The death, in case you were uncooperative, would be for little Resi Noth.'

'Her mission was to make me love her?' I said.

'Yes,' said Wirtanen.

'She did it very well –' I said sadly, 'not that it was hard to do.'

'Sorry to have such news for you,' said Wirtanen.

'It clears up some mysteries – not that I wanted them cleared up,' I said. 'Do you know what she had in her suitcase?'

'Your collected works?' he said.

'You knew about that, too? To think they would go to such pains – to give her props like those! How did they know where to look for those manuscripts?'

'They weren't in Berlin. They were neatly stored in Moscow,' said Wirtanen.

'How did they get there?' I said.

'They were the main evidence in the trial of Stepan Bodovskov,' he said.

'Who?' I said.

'Stepan Bodovskov was a corporal, an interpreter, with the first Russian troops to enter Berlin,' said Wirtanen. 'He found the trunk containing your writings in a theater loft. He took the trunk for booty.'

'Some booty,' I said.

'It turned out to be remarkably fine booty,' said Wirtanen. 'Bodovskov was fluent in German. He went through the contents of the trunk, and he decided that he had a trunkful of instant career.

'He started modestly, translating a few of your poems into Russian, and sending them off to a literary magazine. They were published and praised.

'Bodovskov next tried a play,' said Wirtanen.

'Which one?' I said.

' "The Goblet," ' said Wirtanen. 'Bodovskov translated that into Russian, and he had himself a villa on the Black Sea practically before they'd taken the sandbags down from the windows of the Kremlin.'

'It was produced?' I said.

'Not only was it produced,' said Wirtanen, 'it continues to be produced all over Russia by both amateurs and professionals. "The Goblet" is the "Charley's Aunt" of contemporary Russian theater. You're more alive than you thought, Campbell.'

'My truth goes marching on,' I murmured.

'What?' said Wirtanen.

'I can't even tell you what the plot of "The Goblet" is,' I said.

So Wirtanen told it to me. 'A blindingly pure young maiden,' he said, 'guards the Holy Grail. She will surrender it only to a knight who is as pure as herself. Such a knight comes along, and is pure enough to win the Grail.

'By winning it, he causes the girl to fall in love with him, and he falls in love with her,' said Wirtanen. 'Do I really have to tell you, the author, the rest?'

'It – it's as though Bodovskov really did write it –' I said, 'as though I'm hearing it for the first time.'

'The knight and the girl –' said Wirtanen, continuing the tale, 'they begin to have impure thoughts about each other, tending, involuntarily, to disqualify themselves from any association with the Grail. The heroine urges the hero to flee with the Grail, before he becomes unworthy of it. The hero vows to flee without the Grail, leaving the heroine worthy of continuing to guard it.

'The hero makes their decision for them,' said Wirtanen, 'since they have both become impure in thought. The Holy Grail disappears. And, stunned by this unanswerable proof of their depravity, the two lovers confirm what they firmly believe to be their damnation with a tender night of love.

'The next morning, confident of hell-fire, they promise to give each other so much joy in life that hell-fire will be a very cheap price to pay. The Holy Grail thereupon appears to them, signifying that Heaven does not despise love like theirs.

And then the Grail goes away again, forever, leaving the hero and the heroine to live happily ever after.'

'My God – I *did* write that, didn't I?' I said.

'Stalin was crazy about it,' said Wirtanen.

'And the other plays –?' I said.

'All produced, all well-received,' said Wirtenan.

'But "The Goblet" was Bodovskov's big hit?' I said.

'The book was the biggest hit of all,' said Wirtanen.

'Bodovskov wrote a book?' I said.

'You wrote a book,' said Wirtanen.

'I never did,' I said.

'*Memoirs of a Monogamous Casanova*?' said Wirtanen.

'It was unprintable!' I said.

'A publishing house in Budapest will be amazed to hear that,' said Wirtanen. 'I'd guess they've printed something like a half-million copies.'

'The communists let a book like that be published openly?' I said.

'*Memoirs of a Monogamous Casanova* is a curious little chapter in Russian history,' said Wirtanen. 'It could hardly be published with official approval in Russia – and yet, it was such an attractive, strangely moral piece of pornography, so ideal for a nation suffering from shortages of everything but men and women, that presses in Budapest were somehow encouraged to start printing it – and those presses have, somehow, never been ordered to stop.' Wirtanen winked at me. 'One of the few sly, playful, harmless crimes a Russian can commit at no risk to himself is smuggling home a copy of *Memoirs of a Monogamous Casanova*. And for whom does he smuggle it? To whom is he going to show this hot stuff? To that salty old crony, his wife.

'For years,' said Wirtanen, 'there was only a Russian edition. But now, it is available in Hungarian, Rumanian, Latvian, Estonian, and, most marvelous of all, German again.'

'Bodovskov gets credit as the author?' I said.

'It's common knowledge that Bodovskov wrote it, though

the book carries no credits – publisher, author, and illustrator supposedly unknown.'

'Illustrator?' I said, harrowed by the idea of pictures of Helga and me cavorting in the nude.

'Fourteen plates in lifelike color –' said Wirtanen, 'forty rubles extra.'

'If only it weren't illustrated!' I said to Wirtanen angrily.

'That makes a difference?' he said.

'It's a mutilation!' I said. 'The pictures are bound to mutilate the words. Those words weren't meant to have pictures with them! With pictures, they aren't the same words!'

He shrugged. 'It's pretty much out of your control, I'm afraid,' he said, 'unless you want to declare war on Russia.'

I closed my eyes wincingly. 'What is it they say in the Chicago Stockyards about what they do to a pig?'

'I don't know,' said Wirtanen.

'They boast that they find a use for everything about a pig but his squeal,' I said.

'So?' said Wirtanen.

'That's how I feel right now –' I said, 'like a pig that's been taken apart, who's had experts find a use for every part. By God – I think they even found a use for my squeal! The part of me that wanted to tell the truth got turned into an expert liar! The lover in me got turned into a pornographer! The artist in me got turned into ugliness such as the world has rarely seen before.

'Even my most cherished memories have now been converted into catfood, glue and liverwurst!' I said.

'Which memories are those?' said Wirtanen.

'Of Helga – my Helga,' I said, and I wept. 'Resi killed those, in the interests of the Soviet Union. She made me faithless to those memories, and they can never be the same again.'

I opened my eyes. 'F— all,' I said quietly. 'I suppose the pigs and I should feel honored by those who proved our usefulness. I'm glad about one thing –'

'Oh?' said Wirtanen.

'I'm glad about Bodovskov,' I said. 'I'm glad somebody got to live like an artist with what I once had. You said he was arrested and tried?'

'And shot,' said Wirtanen.

'For plagiarism?' I said.

'For originality,' said Wirtanen. 'Plagiarism is the silliest of misdemeanors. What harm is there in writing what's already been written? Real originality is a capital crime, often calling for cruel and unusual punishment in advance of the *coup de grâce*.'

'I don't understand,' I said.

'Your friend, Kraft-Potapov, realized that you were the author of a lot of things Bodovskov claimed to have written,' said Wirtanen. 'He reported the facts to Moscow. Bodovskov's villa was raided. The magic trunk containing your writings was discovered under straw in the loft in his stable.'

'So –?' I said.

'Every word by you in that trunk had been published,' said Wirtanen.

'And –?' I said.

'Bodovskov had begun to replenish the trunk with magic of his own,' said Wirtanen. 'The police found a two-thousand-page satire on the Red Army, written in a style distinctly un-Bodovskovian. For that un-Bodovskovian behavior, Bodovskov was shot.

'But enough of the past!' said Wirtanen. 'Listen to what I've got to tell you about the future. In about half an hour,' he said, looking at his watch, 'Jones' house is going to be raided. The place is surrounded now. I wanted you out of there, since it's going to be a complicated enough mess as it is.'

'Where do you suggest I go?' I said.

'Don't go back to your flat,' he said. 'Patriots have taken the place apart. They'd probably take you apart, too, if they caught you there.'

'What's going to happen to Resi?' I said.

'Deportation is all,' said Wirtanen. 'She hasn't committed any crimes.'

'And Kraft?' I said.

'A good long stretch in prison,' he said. 'That's no shame. I think he'd rather go to prison than home anyway.

'The Reverend Lionel J. D. Jones, D.D.S., D.D.,' said Wirtanen, 'will go back to prison for illegal possession of fire-arms and whatever else of a straightforward criminal nature we can pin on him. Nothing is planned for Father Keeley, so I imagine he'll drift back to Skid Row again. The Black Fuehrer will be set adrift again, too.'

'And the Iron Guardsmen?' I said.

'The Iron Guardsmen?' I said.

'The Iron Guardsmen of the White Sons of the American Constitution,' said Wirtanen, 'are going to get an impressive lecture on the illegality in this country of private armies, mur-der, mayhem, riots, treason, and violent overthrow of the government. They'll be sent home to educate their parents, if such a thing is possible.'

He looked at his watch again. 'You'd better go now – get clear out of the neighborhood.'

'Can I ask who your agent in Jones' house is?' I said. 'Who was it that slipped the note into my pocket, telling me to come here?'

'You can ask,' said Wirtanen, 'but you must surely know I won't tell you.'

'You don't trust me to that extent?' I said.

'How could I ever trust a man who's been as good a spy as you have?' said Wirtanen. 'Hmm?'

I left Wirtanen.

But I hadn't taken many steps before I understood that the only place I wanted to be was back in Jones' cellar with my mistress and my best friend.

I knew them for what they were, but the fact remained that they were all I had.

I returned by the same route over which I had fled, went in through Jones' coalbin door.

Resi, Father Keeley, and the Black Fuehrer were playing cards when I got back.

Nobody had missed me.

The Iron Guard of the White Sons of the American Constitution was having a class in flag courtesy in the furnace room, a class conducted by one of its own members.

Jones had gone upstairs to write, to create.

Kraft, the Russian Master Spy, was reading a copy of *Life* that had a portrait of Werner von Braun on the cover. Kraft had the magazine open to the center spread, a panorama of a swamp in the Age of Reptiles.

A small radio was playing. It announced a song. The title of the song fixed itself in my mind. This is no miracle of total recall, my remembering the title. The title was apt for the moment – for almost any moment, actually. The title was 'Dat Old Golden Rule.'

At my request, the Haifa Institute for the Documentation of War Criminals has run down the lyric of that song for me. The lyric is as follows:

> Oh, baby, baby, baby,
> Why do you break my heart this way?
> You say you want to go steady,
> But then all you do is stray.

I'm so confused,
I'm not amused,
You make me feel like such a fool.
You smile and lie,
You make me cry.
Why don't you learn dat old Golden Rule?

'What's the game?' I said to the card players.

'Old Maid,' said Father Keeley. He was taking the game seriously. He wanted to win, and I saw that he had the queen of spades, the Old Maid, in his hand.

It might make me seem more human at this point, which is to say more sympathetic, if I were to declare that I itched and blinked and nearly swooned with a feeling of unreality.

Sorry.

Not so.

I confess to a ghastly lack in myself. Anything I see or hear or feel or taste or smell is real to me. I am so much a credulous plaything of my senses that nothing is unreal to me. This armor-plated credulity has been continent even in times when I was struck on the head or drunk or, in one freakish adventure that need not concern this accounting, even under the influence of cocaine.

There in Jones' basement, Kraft showed me the picture of von Braun on the cover of *Life*, asked me if I knew him.

'Von Braun?' I said. 'The Thomas Jefferson of the Space Age? Sure. The Baron danced with my wife once at a birthday party in Hamburg for General Walter Dornberger.'

'Good dancer?' said Kraft.

'Sort of Mickey Mouse dancing –' I said, 'the way all the big Nazis danced, if they had to dance.'

'You think he'd recognize you now?' said Kraft.

'I know he would,' I said. 'I ran into him on Fifty-second Street about a month ago, and he called me by name. He was very shocked to see me in such reduced circumstances. He said he knew a lot of people in the public relations business, and he offered to talk to them about giving me a job.'

'You'd be good at public relations,' said Kraft.

'I certainly don't have any powerful convictions to get in the way of a client's message,' I said.

The game of Old Maid broke up, with Father Keeley the loser, with that pathetic old virgin still stuck with the queen of spades.

'Well,' said Keeley, as though he'd won much in the past, as though a rich future were still his, 'you can't win them all.'

He and the Black Fuehrer went upstairs, pausing each few steps to count to twenty.

And then Resi, Kraft-Potapov and I were alone.

Resi came over to me, put her arm around my waist, laid her cheek against my chest. 'Just think, darling –' she said.

'Hmm?' I said.

'Tomorrow we'll be in Mexico,' she said.

'Um,' I said.

'You seem worried,' she said.

'Me worry?' I said.

'Preoccupied,' she said.

'Do I look preoccupied to you?' I said to Kraft. He was studying the picture of the swamp again.

'No,' he said.

'My good old normal self,' I said.

Kraft pointed to a pterodactyl that was winging over the swamp. 'Who would think a thing like that could fly?' he said.

'Who would ever think that a ramshackle old fart like me would win the heart of such a beautiful girl, and have such a talented, loyal friend besides?' I said.

'I find it very easy to love you,' said Resi. 'I always have.'

'I was just thinking –' I said.

'Tell me your thoughts,' said Resi.

'Maybe Mexico isn't exactly what we want,' I said.

'We can always move on,' said Kraft.

'Maybe – there at the Mexico City airport –' I said, 'maybe we could just get right on a jet –'

Kraft put his magazine down. 'And go where?' he said.

'I don't know,' I said. 'Just go somewhere very fast. I suppose it's the idea of movement that excites me; I've been sitting still so long.'

'Um,' said Kraft.

'Moscow, maybe,' I said.

'What?' said Kraft incredulously.

'Moscow,' I said. 'I'd like very much to see Moscow.'

'That's a novel idea,' said Kraft.

'You don't like it?' I said.

'I – I'll have to think about it,' he said.

Resi started to move away from me, but I held her tight. 'You think about it, too,' I said to her.

'If you want me to,' she said faintly.

'Heaven!' I said, and I jiggled her to make her bubble. 'The more I think about it, the more attractive it becomes,' I said. 'If we only stayed in Mexico City for two minutes between planes, that would be long enough for me.'

Kraft stood up, exercising his fingers elaborately. 'This is a joke?' he said.

'Is it?' I said. 'An old friend like you should be able to tell if I'm joking or not.'

'You must be joking,' he said. 'What is there in Moscow that could interest you?'

'I'd try to locate an old friend of mine,' I said.

'I didn't know you had a friend in Moscow,' he said.

'I don't know that he's in Moscow – just somewhere in Russia,' I said. 'I'd have to make inquiries.'

'What's his name?' said Kraft.

'Stepan Bodovskov –' I said, 'the writer.'

'Oh,' said Kraft. He sat down again, picked up the magazine again.

'You've heard of him?' I said.

'No,' he said.

'What about Colonel Iona Potapov?' I said.

Resi twisted away from me, stood with her back to the farthest wall.

'You know Potapov?' I asked her.

'No,' she said.

'You?' I asked Kraft.

'No,' he said. 'Why don't you tell me about him?'

'He's a communist agent,' I said. 'He's trying to get me to Mexico City so I can be kidnapped and flown to Moscow for trial.'

'No!' said Resi.

'Shut up!' Kraft said to her. He stood, threw the magazine aside. He went for a small pistol he had in his pocket, but I got the drop on him with the Luger.

I made him throw the pistol on the floor.

'Look at us –' he said wonderingly, as though he were an innocent bystander, 'cowboys and Indians.'

'Howard –' said Resi.

'Don't say a word,' Kraft warned her.

'Darling –' said Resi tearfully, 'the dream about Mexico – I thought it was really coming true! We were *all* going to escape!' She opened her arms. 'Tomorrow –' she said weakly.

'Tomorrow –' she whispered again.

And then she went to Kraft, as though she wanted to claw him. But there was no strength in her hands. The hold they took on Kraft was feeble.

'We were all going to be born anew,' she said to him brokenly. 'You, too – you, too. Didn't – didn't you want that for yourself? How could you speak so warmly about the new lives we would have, and still not want them?'

Kraft did not reply.

Resi turned to me. 'I'm a communist agent – yes. And so is he. He *is* Colonel Iona Potapov. And our mission *was* to get you to Moscow. But I wasn't going to go through with it – because I love you, because the love you gave me was the only love I've ever had, the only love I ever will have.

'I told you I wasn't going through with it, didn't I?' she said to Kraft.

'She told me,' said Kraft.

'And he agreed with me,' said Resi. 'And he came up with

this dream of Mexico, where we would *all* get out of the trap – live happily ever after.'

'How did you find out?' Kraft asked me.

'American agents followed the scheme all the way,' I said. 'This place is surrounded now. You're cooked.'

About the raid –

   About Resi Noth –

   About how she died –

   About how she died in my arms, there in the basement of the Reverend Lionel J. D. Jones, D.D.S., D.D. –

   It was wholly unexpected.

   Resi seemed so in favor of life, so right for life, that the possibility of her preferring death did not occur to me.

   I was sufficiently a man of the world, or sufficiently unimaginative – take your choice – to think that a girl that young and pretty and clever would have an entertaining time of it, no matter where fate and politics shoved her next. And, as I pointed out to her, nothing worse than deportation was in store for her.

   'Nothing worse than that?' she said.

   'That's all,' I said. 'I doubt that you'll even have to pay for your passage back.'

   'You're not sorry to see me go?' she said.

   'Certainly, I'm sorry,' I said. 'But there's nothing I can do to keep you with me. Any minute now people are going to come in here and arrest you. You don't expect me to fight them, do you?'

   'You won't fight them?' she said.

   'Of course not,' I said. 'What chance would I have?'

   'That matters?' she said.

   'You mean –' I said, 'why don't I die for love, like a knight in a Howard W. Campbell, Jr., play?'

   'That's exactly what I mean,' she said. 'Why don't we die together, right here and now?'

   I laughed. 'Resi, darling –' I said, 'you have a full life ahead of you.'

   'I have a full life behind me –' she said, 'all in those few sweet hours with you.'

'That sounds like a line I might have written as a young man,' I said.

'It is a line you wrote as a young man,' she said.

'Foolish young man,' I said.

'I adore that young man,' she said.

'When was it you fell in love with him?' I said. 'As a child?'

'As a child – and then as a woman,' she said. 'When they gave me all the things you'd written, told me to study them, that's when I fell in love as a woman.'

'I'm sorry – I can't congratulate you on your literary tastes,' I said.

'You no longer believe that love is the only thing to live for?' she said.

'No,' I said.

'Then tell me what to live for – anything at all,' she said beseechingly. 'It doesn't have to be love. Anything at all!' She gestured at objects around the shabby room, dramatizing exquisitely my own sense of the world's being a junk shop. 'I'll live for that chair, that picture, that furnace pipe, that couch, that crack in the wall! Tell me to live for it, and I will!' she cried.

It was now me that her strengthless hands laid hold of. She closed her eyes, wept. 'It doesn't have to be love,' she whispered. 'Just tell me what it should be.'

'Resi –' I said gently.

'*Tell me!*' she said, and strength came into her hands, did tender violence to my clothes.

'I'm an old man –' I said helplessly. It was a coward's lie. I am not an old man.

'All right, old man – tell me what to live for,' she said. 'Tell me what you live for, so I can live for it, too – here or ten thousand kilometers from here! Tell me why you want to go on being alive, so I can go on wanting to be alive, too!'

And then the raiders broke in.

The forces of law and order plunged in through every door, waving guns, blowing whistles, shining dazzling lights where there was plenty of light already.

There was a small army of them, and they exclaimed over all the melodramatically evil goodies in the cellar. They exclaimed like children around a Christmas tree.

A dozen of them, all young, apple-cheeked and virtuous, surrounded Resi, Kraft-Potapov and me, took my Luger away from me, turned us into rag dolls as they ransacked us for other weapons.

More raiders came down the stairs prodding the Reverend Dr. Lionel J. D. Jones, the Black Fuehrer, and Father Keeley before them.

Dr. Jones stopped halfway down the stairs, confronted his tormentors. 'All I've done,' he said majestically, 'is do what you people should be doing.'

'What should we be doing?' said a G-man. He was obviously in command of the raid.

'Protecting the Republic,' said Jones. 'Why bother us? Everything we do is to make the country stronger! Join with us, and let's go after the people who are trying to make it weaker!'

'Who's that?' said the G-man.

'I have to tell you?' said Jones. 'Haven't you even found that out in the course of your work? The Jews! The Catholics! The Negroes! The Orientals! The Unitarians! The foreign-born, who don't have any understanding of democracy, who play right into the hands of the socialists, the communists, the anarchists, the anti-Christs and the Jews!'

'For your information,' said the G-man in cool triumph, 'I am a Jew.'

'That proves what I've just been saying!' said Jones.

'How's that?' said the G-man.

'The Jews have infiltrated everything!' said Jones, smiling the smile of a logician who could never be topped.

'You talk about the Catholics and the Negroes —' said the G-man, 'and yet, here your two best friends are a Catholic and a Negro.'

'What's so mysterious about that?' said Jones.

'Don't you hate them?' said the G-man.

'Certainly not,' said Jones. 'We all believe the same basic thing.'

'What's that?' said the G-man.

'This once-proud country of ours is falling into the hands of the wrong people,' said Jones. He nodded, and so did Father Keeley and the Black Fuehrer. 'And, before it gets back on the right track,' said Jones, 'some heads are going to roll.'

I have never seen a more sublime demonstration of the totalitarian mind, a mind which might be likened unto a system of gears where teeth have been filed off at random. Such snaggle-toothed thought machine, driven by a standard or even by a substandard libido, whirls with the jerky, noisy, gaudy pointlessness of a cuckoo clock in Hell.

The boss G-man concluded wrongly that there were no teeth on the gears in the mind of Jones. 'You're completely crazy,' he said.

Jones wasn't completely crazy. The dismaying thing about the classic totalitarian mind is that any given gear, though mutilated, will have at its circumference unbroken sequences of teeth that are immaculately maintained, that are exquisitely machined.

Hence the cuckoo clock in Hell – keeping perfect time for eight minutes and twenty-three seconds, jumping ahead fourteen minutes, keeping perfect time for six seconds, jumping ahead two seconds, keeping perfect time for two hours and one second, then jumping ahead a year.

The missing teeth, of course, are simple, obvious truths, truths available and comprehensible even to ten-year-olds, in most cases.

The wilful filing off of gear teeth, the wilful doing without certain obvious pieces of information –

That was how a household as contradictory as one composed of Jones, Father Keeley, Vice-Bundesfuehrer Krapptauer, and the Black Fuehrer could exist in relative harmony –

That was how my father-in-law could contain in one mind an indifference toward slave women and love for a blue vase –

That was how Rudolf Hoess, Commandant of Auschwitz,

could alternate over the loudspeakers of Auschwitz great music and calls for corpse-carriers –

That was how Nazi Germany could sense no important differences between civilization and hydrophobia –

That is the closest I can come to explaining the legions, the nations of lunatics I've seen in my time. And for me to attempt such a mechanical explanation is perhaps a reflection of the father whose son I was. *Am.* When I pause to think about it, which is rarely, I am, after all, the son of an engineer.

Since there is no one else to praise me, I will praise myself – will say that I have never tampered with a single tooth in my thought machine, such as it is. There are teeth missing, God knows – some I was born without, teeth that will never grow. And other teeth have been stripped by the clutchless shifts of history –

But never have I wilfully destroyed a tooth on a gear of my thinking machine. Never have I said to myself, 'This fact I can do without.'

Howard W. Campbell, Jr., praises himself! There's life in the old boy yet!

And, where there's life –

There is life.

'My only regret,' Dr. Jones said to the boss G-man there on the cellar stairs, 'is that I have but one life to give to my country.'

'We'll see if we can't dig up some other regrets for you, too,' said the boss.

Now the Iron Guard of the White Sons of the American Constitution crowded in from the furnace room. Some of the guardsmen were hysterical. The paranoia their parents had been inculcating for years had suddenly paid off. Here was persecution!

One youth clutched the staff on an American flag. He waved it back and forth, banging the eagle on the tip of the staff against overhead pipes.

'This is your country's flag!' he cried.

'We already know that,' said the boss B-man. 'Take it away from him!'

'This day will go down in history!' said Jones.

'Every day goes down in history,' said the boss. 'All right ,' he said, 'where's the man who calls himself George Kraft?'

Kraft raised his hand. He did it almost cheerfully.

'Is that *your* country's flag, too?' said the boss wryly.

'I'd have to look at it more closely,' said Kraft.

'How does it feel to have such a long and distinguished career come to an end?' the boss asked Kraft.

'All careers do end,' said Kraft. 'That's something I've known for a long time.'

'Maybe they'll make a movie of your life,' said the boss.

Kraft smiled. 'Maybe,' he said. 'I would want a lot of money for the rights.'

'There's only one actor who could really play the part, though,' said the boss. 'He might be hard to get.'

'Oh?' said Kraft. 'Who is that?'

'Charlie Chaplin,' said the boss. 'Who else could play a

spy who was steadily drunk from 1941 until 1948? Who else could play a Russian spy who built an apparatus composed almost entirely of American agents?'

Kraft's urbanity dropped away, revealing him as a pale and puckered old man. 'That's not true!' he said.

'Ask your superiors, if you don't believe me,' said the boss.

'They know?' said Kraft.

'They finally caught on,' said the boss. 'You were on your way home to a bullet in the back of your neck.'

'Why did you save me?' said Kraft.

'Call it sentimentality,' said the boss.

Kraft thought his situation over, and schizophrenia rescued him neatly. 'None of this really concerns me,' he said, and his urbanity returned.

'Why not?' said the boss.

'Because I'm a painter,' said Kraft. 'That's the main thing I am.'

'Be sure to bring your paintbox to prison,' said the boss. He switched his attention to Resi. 'You, of course, are Resi Noth,' he said.

'Yes,' she said.

'Have you enjoyed your little stay in our country?' said the boss.

'What am I supposed to say?' said Resi.

'Anything you like,' said the boss. 'If you have any complaints, I'll pass them on to the proper authorities. We're trying to increase the tourist trade from Europe, you know.'

'You say very funny things,' she said unsmilingly. 'I am sorry I can't say funny things back. This is not a funny time for me.'

'I'm sorry to hear that,' said the boss lightly.

'You aren't sorry,' said Resi. 'I am the only person who is sorry.

'I am sorry I have nothing to live for,' said Resi. 'All I have is love for one man, but that man does not love me. He is so used up that he can't love any more. There is nothing left of him but curiosity and a pair of eyes.

'I can't say anything funny,' said Resi. 'But I can show you something interesting.'

Resi seemed to dab her lip with a finger. What she really did was put a little capsule of cyanide in her mouth.

'I will show you a woman who dies for love,' she said.

Right then and there, Resi Noth pitched into my arms, stone dead.

I was arrested along with everyone else in the house. I was released within an hour, thanks, I suppose, to the intercession of my Blue Fairy Godmother. The place where I was held so briefly was an unmarked office in the Empire State Building.

An agent took me down on an elevator and out onto the sidewalk, restoring me to the mainstream of life. I took perhaps fifty steps down the sidewalk, and then I stopped.

I froze.

It was not guilt that froze me. I had taught myself never to feel guilt.

It was not a ghastly sense of loss that froze me. I had taught myself to covet nothing.

It was not a loathing of death that froze me. I had taught myself to think of death as a friend.

It was not heartbroken rage against injustice that froze me. I had taught myself that a human being might as well look for diamond tiaras in the gutter as for rewards and punishments that were fair.

It was not the thought that I was so unloved that froze me. I had taught myself to do without love.

It was not the thought that God was cruel that froze me. I had taught myself never to expect anything from Him.

What froze me was the fact that I had absolutely no reason to move in any direction. What had made me move through so many dead and pointless years was curiosity.

Now even that had flickered out.

How long I stood frozen there, I cannot say. If I was ever going to move again, someone else was going to have to furnish the reason for moving.

Somebody did.

A policeman watched me for a while, and then he came over to me, and he said, 'You all right?'

'Yes,' I said.

'You've been standing here a long time,' he said.
'I know,' I said.
'You waiting for somebody?' he said.
'No,' I said.
'Better move on, don't you think?' he said.
'Yes, sir,' I said.
And I moved on.

41: Chemicals . . .

From the Empire State Building I walked downtown. I walked all the way to my old home in Greenwich Village, to Resi's and my and Kraft's old home.

I smoked cigarettes all the way, began to think of myself as a lightning bug.

I encountered many fellow lightning bugs. Sometimes I gave the cherry red signal first, sometimes they. And I left the seashell roar and the aurora borealis of the city's heart farther and farther behind me.

The hour was late. I began to catch signals of fellow lightning bugs trapped in upper stories.

Somewhere a siren, a tax-supported mourner, wailed.

When I got at last to my building, my home, all windows were dark save one on the second floor, one window in the apartment of young Dr. Abraham Epstein.

He, too, was a lightning bug.

He glowed; I glowed back.

Somewhere a motorcycle started up, sounded like a string of firecrackers.

A black cat crossed between me and the door of the building. 'Ralph?' it said.

The entrance hall of the building was dark, too. The ceiling light did not respond to the switch. I struck a match, saw that the mailboxes had all been broken into.

In the wavering light of the match and the formless surroundings, the bent and gaping doors of the mailboxes might have been the doors of cells in a jail in a burning city somewhere.

My match attracted a patrolman. He was young and lonesome.

'What are you doing here?' he said.

'I live here,' I said. 'This is my home.'

'Any identification?' he said.

So I gave him some identification, told him the attic was mine.

'You're the reason for all this trouble,' he said. He wasn't scolding me. He was simply interested.

'If you say so,' I said.

'I'm surprised you came back,' he said.

'I'll go away again,' I said.

'I can't order you to go away,' he said. 'I'm just surprised you came back.'

'It's all right for me to go upstairs?' I said.

'It's your home,' he said. 'Nobody can keep you out of it.'

'Thank you,' I said.

'Don't thank me,' he said. 'It's a free country, and everybody gets protected exactly alike.' He said this pleasantly. He was giving me a lesson in civics.

'That's certainly the way to run a country,' I said.

'I don't know if you're kidding me or not,' he said, 'but that's right.'

'I'm not kidding you,' I said. 'I swear I'm not.' This simple oath of allegiance satisfied him.

'My father was killed in Iwo Jima,' he said.

'I'm sorry,' I said.

'I guess there were good people killed on both sides,' he said.

'I think that's true,' I said.

'You think there'll be another one?' he said.

'Another what?' I said.

'Another war,' he said.

'Yes,' I said.

'Me too,' he said. 'Isn't that hell?'

'You chose the right word,' I said.

'What can any one person do?' he said.

'Each person does a little something,' I said, 'and there you are.'

He sighed heavily. 'It all adds up,' he said. 'People don't realize.' He shook his head. 'What should people do?'

'Obey the laws,' I said.

'They don't even want to do that, half of 'em,' he said. 'The things I see – the things people say to me. Sometimes I get very discouraged.'

'Everybody does that from time to time,' I said.

'I guess it's partly chemistry,' he said.

'What is?' I said.

'Getting down in the dumps,' he said. 'Isn't that what they're finding out – that a lot of that's chemicals?'

'I don't know,' I said.

'That's what I read,' he said. 'That's one of the things they're finding out.'

'Very interesting,' I said.

'They can give a man certain chemicals, and he goes crazy,' he said. 'That's one of the things they're working with. Maybe it's all chemicals.'

'Very possible,' I said.

'Maybe its different chemicals that different countries eat that makes people act in different ways at different times,' he said.

'I'd never thought of that before,' I said.

'Why else would people change so much?' he said. 'My brother was over in Japan, and he said the Japanese were the nicest people he ever met, and it was the Japanese who'd killed our father! Think about that for a minute.'

'All right,' I said.

'It *has* to be chemicals, doesn't it?' he said.

'I see what you mean,' I said.

'Sure,' he said. 'You think about it some more.'

'All right,' I said.

'I think about chemicals all the time,' he said. 'Sometimes I think I should go back to school and find out all the things they've found out so far about chemicals.'

'I think you should,' I said.

'Maybe, when they find out more about chemicals,' he said, 'there won't have to be policemen or wars or crazy houses or divorces or drunks or juvenile delinquents or women gone bad or anything any more.'

154

'That would sure be nice,' I said.

'It's possible,' he said.

'I believe you,' I said.

'The way they're going, everything's possible now, if they just work at it – get the money and get the smartest people and get to work. Have a crash program,' he said.

'I'm for it,' I said.

'Look how some women go half off their nut once a month,' he said. 'Certain chemicals get loose, and the women can't help but act that way. Sometimes a certain chemical will get loose after a woman's had a baby, and she'll kill the baby. That happened four doors down from here just last week.'

'How awful,' I said. 'I hadn't heard –'

'Most unnatural thing a woman can do is kill her own baby, but she did it,' he said. 'Certain chemicals in the blood made her do it, even though she knew better, didn't want to do it at all.'

'Um,' I said.

'You wonder what's wrong with the world –' he said, 'well, there's an important clue right there.'

I went upstairs to my ratty attic, went up the oak and plaster snail of the stairwell.

While the column of air enclosed by the stairs had carried in the past a melancholy freight of coal dust and cooking smells and the sweat of plumbing, that air was cold and sharp now. Every window in my attic had been broken. All warm gases had been whisked up the stairwell and out my windows, as though up a whistling flue.

The air was clean.

The feeling of a stale old building suddenly laid open, an infected atmosphere lanced, made clean, was familiar to me. I had felt it often enough in Berlin. Helga and I were bombed out twice. Both times there was a staircase left to climb.

One time we climbed the stairs to a roofless and windowless home, a home otherwise magically undisturbed. Another time, we climbed the stairs to cold thin air, two floors below where home had been.

Both moments at those splintered stairheads under the open sky were exquisite.

The exquisiteness went on for only a short time, naturally, for, like any human family, we loved our nests and needed them. But, for a minute or two, anyway, Helga and I felt like Noah and his wife on Mount Ararat.

There is no better feeling than that.

And then the air-raid sirens blew again, and we realized that we were ordinary people, without dove or covenant, and that the flood, far from being over, had scarcely begun.

I remember one time, when Helga and I went from the head of a splintered staircase in the sky down into a shelter deep in the ground, and the big bombs walked all around above. And they walked and they walked and they walked, and it seemed that they never would go away.

And the shelter was long and narrow, like a railroad car, and it was full.

And there was a man, a woman, and their three children on the bench facing Helga and me. And the woman started speaking to the ceiling, the bombs, the airplanes, the sky, and to God Almighty above all that.

She started softly, but she wasn't talking to anybody in the shelter itself.

'All right –' she said, 'here we are. We're right down here. We hear you up there. We hear how angry you are.' The loudness of her voice jumped sharply.

'Dear God, how angry you are!' she cried.

Her husband – a haggard civilian with a patch over one eye, with the recognition button of the Nazi teachers' union on his lapel – spoke to her warningly.

She did not hear him.

'What is it you want us to do?' she said to the ceiling and all that lay above. 'Whatever it is you want us to do,' she said, 'tell us, and we'll do it!'

A bomb crashed down close by, shook loose from the ceiling a snowfall of calcimine, brought the woman to her feet shrieking, and her husband with her.

'We surrender! We give up!' she yelled, and great relief and happiness spread over her face. 'You can stop now,' she yelled. She laughed. 'We quit! It's over!' She turned to tell the good news to her children.

Her husband knocked her cold.

That one-eyed teacher set her down on the bench, propped her against the wall. And then he went to the highest-ranking person present, a vice-admiral, as it happened. 'She's a woman ... hysterical ... they get hysterical ... she doesn't mean it ... she has the Golden Order of Parenthood ...' he said to the vice-admiral.

The vice-admiral wasn't baffled or annoyed. He didn't feel miscast. With fine dignity, he gave the man absolution. 'It's all right,' he said. 'It's understandable. Don't worry.'

The teacher marveled at a system that could forgive weakness. '*Heil Hitler*,' he said, bowing as he backed away.

'*Heil Hitler*,' said the vice-admiral.

The teacher now began to revive his wife. He had good news for her – that she was forgiven, that everyone understood.

And all the time the bombs walked and walked overhead, and the schoolteacher's three children did not bat an eye.

Nor, I thought, would they ever.

Nor, I thought, would I.

Ever again.

The door of my ratty attic had been torn off its hinges, had disappeared entirely. In its place the janitor had tacked a pup-tent of mine, and over the pup-tent a zigzag of boards. He had written on the zigzag boards, in gold radiator paint that reflected the light of my match:

'Nobody and nothing inside.'

Be that as it may, somebody had since ripped a bottom corner of the canvas free of its tacks, giving my ratty attic a small, triangular flap-door, like a tepee.

I crawled in.

The light switch in my attic did not respond, either. What light there was came through the few unbroken window panes. The broken panes had been replaced with wads of paper, rags, clothes and bedding. Night winds whistled around these wads. What light there was was blue.

I looked out through the back windows by the stove, looked down into the foreshortened enchantment of the little private park below, the little Eden formed of joined back yards. No one was playing in it now.

There was no one in it to cry, as I should have liked someone to cry:

'Olly-olly-ox-in-freeeeeee.'

There was a stir, a rustle in the shadow of my attic. I imagined it to be the rustle of a rat.

I was wrong.

It was the rustle of Bernard B. O'Hare, the man who had captured me so long ago. It was the stir of my own personal Fury, the man who perceived his noblest aspect in his loathing and hounding of me.

I do not mean to slander him by associating the sound he made with the sound of a rat. I do not think of O'Hare as a rat, though his actions with regard to me had the same nagging irrelevance as the rats' scrabbling passions in my attic walls. I didn't really know O'Hare, and I didn't want to know him. The fact of his having put me under arrest in Germany was a fact of submicroscopic interest to me. He wasn't my nemesis. My game was up long before O'Hare took me into custody. To me, O'Hare was simply one more gatherer of wind-blown trash in the tracks of war.

O'Hare had a far more exciting view of what we were to each other. When drunk, at any rate, he thought of himself as St. George and of me as the dragon.

When I first saw him in the shadows of my attic, he was seated on a galvanised bucket turned upside down. He was in the uniform of the American Legion. He had a quart of whisky with him. He had apparently been waiting for me a long time, drinking and smoking the while. He was drunk, but he had kept his uniform neat. His tie was straight. His cap was on and set at the proper angle. The uniform was important to him, was supposed to be important to me, too.

'Know who I am?' he said.

'Yes,' I said.

'I'm not as young as I was once,' he said. 'Haven't changed much, have I?'

'No,' I said. I've described him earlier in this account as having looked like a lean young wolf. When I saw him in my attic, he looked unhealthy – pale and stringy and hot-eyed. He had become less wolf than coyote, I thought. His post-war years had not been years of merry blooming.

'Expecting me?' he said.

'You told me I could,' I said. I had to be polite and careful with him. I supposed correctly that he meant to hurt me. The fact that he was in a very neat uniform, and that he was smaller and much lighter than me, suggested that he had a weapon on him somewhere – most likely a gun.

He now got off the bucket, showing me, in his ramshackle rising, how drunk he was. He knocked the bucket over in the process.

160

He grinned. 'Ever have nightmares about me, Campbell?' he said.

'Often,' I said. It was a lie, of course.

'Surprised I didn't bring anybody with me?' he said.

'Yes,' I said.

'Plenty of people wanted to come along,' he said. 'There was a whole bunch wanted to come down with me from Boston. And after I got to New York this afternoon, I went into a bar and got talking to some strangers, and they asked if they could come along, too.'

'Um,' I said.

'And you know what I said to them?' he asked me.

'Nope,' I said.

'I said to them, "Sorry, boys — but this is a party just for Campbell and me. That's the way it's got to be — just the two of us, face to face," ' he said.

'Um,' I said.

' "This thing's been a-building over the years," I told 'em,' said O'Hare. ' "It's in the stars —" I told 'em, "in the stars that Howard Campbell and me meet again after all these years." Don't you feel that way?' he asked me.

'What way?' I said.

'It's in the stars,' he said. 'We had to meet like this, right here in this very room, and neither one of us could have avoided it if we'd tried.'

'Possibly,' I said.

'Just when you think there isn't any point to life —' he said, 'then, all of a sudden, you realize you are being aimed right straight at something.'

'I know what you mean,' I said.

He swayed, steadied himself. 'You know what I do for a living?' he said.

'No,' I said.

'Dispatcher for frozen-custard trucks,' he said.

'Pardon me?' I said.

'Fleet of trucks goes around to factories, beaches, ballgames

– anywhere there's people –' O'Hare seemed to forget all about me for a few seconds, to reflect murkily on the mission of the trucks he dispatched. 'Custard machine's right there on the truck,' he murmured. 'Two flavors is all – chocolate and vanilla.' His mood was exactly what poor Resi's mood had been when she told me about the ghastly pointlessness of her job at a cigarette-making machine in Dresden.

'When the war ended,' O'Hare said to me, 'I expected to be a lot more in fifteen years than a dispatcher of frozen-custard trucks.'

'I guess we've all had disappointments,' I said.

He didn't respond to this feeble try at brotherhood. His concern was for himself alone. 'I was going to be a doctor, I was going to be a lawyer, a writer, an architect, an engineer, a newspaper reporter –' he said. 'There wasn't anything I couldn't be,' he said.

'And then I got married –' he said, 'and the wife started having kids right away, and I opened a damn diaper service with a buddy, and the buddy ran off with the money, and the wife kept having kids. After the diaper service it was Venetian blinds, and after the Venetian-blind business went bust, it was frozen custard. And all the time the wife was having more kids, and the damn car breaking down, and bill-collectors coming around, and termites boiling out of the baseboards every night spring and fall.'

'Sorry,' I said.

'And I asked myself,' said O'Hare, 'what does it mean? Where do I fit in? What's the point of any of it?'

'Good questions,' I said softly, and I put myself close to a pair of heavy fire-tongs.

'And then somebody sent me a copy of that newspaper with the story of how you were still alive,' said O'Hare, and he re-lived for me the cruel excitement the story had given him. 'And then it hit me –' he said, 'why I was alive, and what the main thing was I was supposed to do.'

He took a step toward me, his eyes wide. 'Here I come, Campbell, out of the past!'

'How do you do?' I said.

'You know what you are to me, Campbell?' he said.

'No,' I said.

'You're pure evil,' he said. 'You're absolutely pure evil.'

'Thank you,' I said.

'You're right – it *is* a kind of compliment,' he said. 'Uusually a bad man's got some good in him – almost as much good as evil. But you –' he said, 'you're the pure thing. For all the good there is in you, you might as well be the Devil.'

'Maybe I am the devil,' I said.

'Don't think I haven't thought of that,' he said.

'What do you plan to do to me?' I asked him.

'Take you apart,' he said, rocking back and forth on the balls of his feet, rolling his shoulders, loosening them. 'When I heard you were alive, I knew it was something I had to do. There wasn't any way out,' he said. 'It had to end like this.'

'I don't see why,' I said.

'Then, by God, I'll show you why,' he said. 'I'll show you, by God, I was born just to take you apart, right here and now.' He called me a yellow-belly. He called me a Nazi. And then he called me the most offensive compound word in the English language.

So I broke his good right arm with the fire-tongs.

That is the only violent act I ever committed in what has now been a long, long life. I met O'Hare in single combat, and I beat him. Beating him was easy. O'Hare was so drugged by booze and fantasies of good triumphing over evil that he hadn't expected me to defend myself.

When he realized that he'd been hit, that the dragon meant to give St. George a real tussle, he looked very surprised.

'So that's the way you want to play –' he said.

And then the agony of a multiple fracture suffused his nervous system, and tears came to his eyes.

'Get out,' I said. 'Or do you want me to break your other arm, and your head, too?' I put the tip of the fire-tongs by his

163

right temple, and I said, 'And I'll take the gun or the knife or whatever it is before you go.'

He shook his head. The pain was so awful that he could not speak.

'You're not armed?' I said.

He shook his head again. 'Fair fight,' he said thickly. 'Fair.'

I patted his pockets, and there weren't any weapons on him. St. George had expected to take the dragon apart with his bare hands!

'You poor, silly, drunk, one-armed sonofabitch!' I said. I tore down the tent in my doorway, kicked out the zigzag of boards. I shoved O'Hare through the opening, onto the landing outside.

The railing stopped O'Hare, and he gazed down the stairwell, down a beckoning helix to the patch of sure death below.

'I'm not your destiny, or the Devil, either!' I said. 'Look at you! Came to kill evil with your bare hands, and now away you go with no more glory than a man sideswiped by a Greyhound bus! And that's all the glory you deserve!' I said. 'That's all that any man at war with pure evil deserves.

'There are plenty of good reasons for fighting,' I said, 'but no good reason ever to hate without reservation, to imagine that God Almighty Himself hates with you, too. Where's evil? It's that large part of every man that wants to hate without limit, that wants to hate with God on his side. It's that part of every man that finds all kinds of ugliness so attractive.

'It's that part of an imbecile,' I said, 'that punishes and vilifies and makes war gladly.'

Whether it was my words or humiliation or booze or surgical shock that made O'Hare throw up, I do not know. Throw up he did. He flashed the hash down the stairwell from four stories up.

'Clean it up,' I said.

He faced me, his eyes still filled with undiluted hatred. 'I'll get you yet, brother,' he said.

'That may be,' I said. 'But it won't change your destiny of

164

bankruptcies, frozen-custard, too many children, termites, and
no cash. If you want to be a soldier in the Legion of God so
much,' I told him, 'try the Salvation Army.'

And O'Hare went away.

44: 'Kahm-boo...'

It is a common experience among jailbirds to wake up and wonder why they are in jail. A theory I propose to myself on such occasions is that I am in jail because I could not bring myself to walk through or leap over another man's vomit. I am referring to the vomit of Bernard B. O'Hare on the foyer floor at the foot of the stairwell.

I left my attic shortly after O'Hare did. There was nothing to keep me there. I took a memento with me, quite by accident. As I left my attic, I kicked something over the threshold and onto the landing. I picked it up. It was a pawn from the chess set I had carved from a broom handle.

I put it in my pocket. I have it still. As I slipped it into my pocket, the stench of the public nuisance O'Hare had created reached me.

As I descended the stairs, the stench grew worse.

When I reached the landing outside the door of young Dr. Abraham Epstein, a man who had spent his childhood in Auschwitz, the stench stopped me.

The next thing I knew, I was knocking on Dr. Epstein's door.

The Doctor came to the door in bathrobe and pajamas. His feet were bare. He was startled to see me.

'Yes?' he said.

'Could I come in?' I said.

'This is a medical matter?' he said. There was a chain across the door.

'No,' I said. 'Personal – political.'

'It can wait?' he said.

'I'd rather it didn't,' I said.

'Give me an idea of what this is all about,' he said.

'I want to go to Israel to stand trial,' I said.

'You what?' he said.

'I want to be tried for my crimes against humanity,' I said. 'I'm willing to go.'

'Why come to me?' he said.

'I thought you might know somebody – somebody who'd like to be notified,' I said.

'I'm not a representative of Israel,' he said. 'I'm an Amercan. Tomorrow you can find all the Israelis you want.'

'I'd like to surrender to an Auschwitzer,' I said.

This made him mad. 'Then find one who thinks about Auschwitz all the time!' he said. 'There are plenty who think about nothing else. I *never* think about it!'

And he slammed the door.

I froze again, frustrated in the one purpose I'd been able to imagine for myself. What Epstein had said about Israelis being available in the morning was surely true –

But there was still the night to get through, and I could not move.

Epstein talked to his mother inside. They talked in German.

I heard only bits of what they said. Epstein was telling his mother what had just happened.

One thing I did hear that impressed me was their use of my name, the sound of my last name.

'Kahm-boo,' they said again and again. That was Campbell to them.

That was the undiluted evil in me, the evil that had had its effect on millions, the disgusting creature good people wanted dead and underground –

'Kahm-boo.'

Epstein's mother got so excited about Kahm-boo and what he was up to now, that she came to the door. I'm sure that she did not expect to see Kahm-boo himself. She wanted only to loathe and wonder at the air he had lately displaced.

She opened the door, her son right behind her, telling her not to do it. She almost fainted at the sight of Kahm-boo himself, Kahm-boo in a state of catalepsis.

Epstein pushed her aside, came out as though to attack me.

'What do you think you're doing?' he said. 'Get the hell away from here!'

When I did not move, did not reply, did not even blink, did not even seem to breathe, he began to understand that I was a medical problem after all.

'Oh, for Christ's sake!' he lamented.

Like a friendly robot, I let him lead me inside. He took me back into the kitchen area of his flat, sat me down at a white table there.

'Can you hear me?' he said.

'Yes,' I said.

'Do you know who I am – where you are?' he said.

'Yes,' I said.

'Have you ever been like this before?' he said.

'No,' I said.

'You need a psychiatrist,' he said. 'I'm no psychiatrist.'

'I told you what I need,' I said. 'Call up somebody – not a psychiatrist. Call up somebody who wants to give me a trial.'

Epstein and his mother, a very old woman, argued back and forth about what to do with me. His mother understood my illness immediately, that it was my world rather than myself that was diseased.

'This is not the first time you've seen eyes like that,' she said to her son in German, 'not the first man you've seen who could not move unless someone told him where to move, who longed for someone to tell him what to do next, who would do anything anyone told him to do next. You saw thousands of them at Auschwitz.'

'I don't remember,' said Epstein tautly.

'All right –' said his mother, 'then let *me* remember. I can remember. Every minute I can remember.

'And, as one who remembers,' said his mother, 'let me say that what he asks for he should have. Call someone.'

'Who will I call?' said Epstein. 'I'm not a Zionist. I'm an anti-Zionist. I'm not even that. I never think about it. I'm a physician. I don't know anybody who's still looking for revenge. I have nothing but contempt for them. Go away. You've come to the wrong place.'

'Call somebody,' said his mother.

'You still want revenge?' he asked her.

'Yes,' she said.

He put his face close to mine. 'And you really want to be punished?' he said.

'I want to be tried,' I said.

'It's all play-acting,' he said, exasperated with both of us. 'It proves nothing!'

'Call somebody,' said his mother.

Epstein threw up his hands. 'All right! All right! I will call Sam. I will tell him he can be a great Zionist hero. He always wanted to be a great Zionist hero.'

What Sam's last name was I never found out. Dr. Epstein called him from the front room of the flat while I remained in the kitchen with Epstein's old mother.

His mother sat down at the table, faced me, rested her arms on the table, studied my face with melancholy curiosity and satisfaction.

'They took all the light bulbs,' she said to me in German.

'What?' I said.

'The people who broke into your apartment – they took all the light bulbs from the stairway,' she said.

'Um,' I said.

'In Germany, too,' she said.

'Pardon me?' I said.

'That was one of the things – when the S.S. or the Gestapo came and took somebody away –' she said.

'I don't understand,' I said.

'Other people would come into the building, wanting to do something patriotic,' she said. 'And that was one of the things they always did. Somebody always took the light bulbs.' She shook her head. 'Such a strange thing for somebody always to do.'

Dr. Epstein came back into the kitchen dusting his hands. 'All right –' he said, 'three heroes will be here shortly – a tailor, a watchmaker, and a pediatrician – all delighted to play the part of Israeli parachutists.'

'Thank you,' I said.

The three came for me in about twenty minutes. They had no weapons, and no status as agents of Israel or as agents of anything but themselves. The only status they had was what my infamy and my anxiousness to surrender to somebody, to almost anybody, gave them.

What my arrest amounted to was a bed for the rest of the night – in the tailor's apartment, as it happened. The next morning, the three surrendered me, with my permission, to Israeli officials.

When the three came for me at Dr. Epstein's apartment, they banged on the front door loudly.

The instant they did that, I felt enormously relieved. I felt happy.

'You're all right now?' said Epstein, before he let them in.

'Yes, thank you, Doctor,' I said.

'You still want to go?' he said.

'Yes,' I said.

'He *has* to go,' said his mother. And then she leaned closer to me, across the kitchen table. She crooned something in German, made it sound like a fragment of a ditty remembered from a happy childhood.

What she crooned was this, a command she had heard over the loudspeakers of Auschwitz – had heard many times a day for years.

'*Leichenträger zur Wache,*' she crooned.

A beautiful language, isn't it?

Translation?

'Corpse-carriers to the guardhouse.'

That's what that old woman crooned to me.

So here I am in Israel, of my own free will, though my cell is locked and my guards have guns.

My story is told, and none too soon – for tomorrow my trial begins. The hare of history once more overtakes the tortoise of art. There will be no more time for writing. Adventuring I must go again.

There are many to testify against me. None to testify for me.

The prosecution intends to begin, I'm told, by playing recordings of the worst of my broadcasts, so the most pitiless witness against me will be myself.

Bernard B. O'Hare is in town at his own expense, annoying the prosecution with the feverish irrelevance of all he has to say.

So, too, is Heinz Schildknecht, my erstwhile best friend and doubles partner, the man whose motorcycle I stole. My lawyer says that Heinz is full of venom for me, and that Heinz, surprisingly, will make a credible witness. Whence this respectability for Heinz, who, after all, worked at a desk next to mine in the Ministry of Propaganda and Popular Enlightenment?

Surprise: Heinz is a Jew, a member of the anti-Nazi underground during the war, an Israeli agent after the war and up to the present time.

And he can prove it.

Good for Heinz!

Dr. Lionel J. D. Jones, D.D.S., D.D., and Iona Potapov *alias* George Kraft, can't come to my trial, both serving in a United States Federal Prison, as they are. They have both sent affidavits, however.

The affidavits of Dr. Jones and Kraft-Potapov aren't much help, to say the least.

Dr. Jones declares under oath that I am a saint and a martyr in the holy Nazi cause. He says, too, that I have the most perfect set of Aryan teeth he's ever seen outside of photographs of Hitler.

Kraft-Potapov declares under oath that Russian intelligence was never able to turn up any proof that I was an ardent Nazi, but that I shouldn't be held responsible for my acts, since I was a political idiot, an artist who could not distinguish between reality and dreams.

The three men who took me into custody in Dr. Epstein's apartment are on hand for the trial – the tailor, the watchmaker, and the pediatrician – on an even more bootless junket than Bernard B. O'Hare's.

Howard W. Campbell, Jr – this is your life!

My Israeli lawyer, Mr. Alvin Dobrowitz, has had all my New York mail forwarded here, hoping unreasonably to find in that mail some proof of my innocence.

Hi ho.

Three letters came today.

I shall open them now, reporting their contents one by one.

Hope springs eternal, they say, in the human breast. It springs eternal, at any rate, in the breast of Dobrowitz, which is, I suppose, why he costs so much.

All that I need to be a free man, says Dobrowitz, is the barest proof that there was such a person as Frank Wirtanen, and that Wirtanen made me an American spy.

Well now – about the letters for today:

The first starts off warmly enough. 'Dear Friend' it calls me, in spite of all the evil things I am said to have done. It assumes that I am a teacher. I explained in an earlier chapter, I believe, how my name happened to find its way onto a list of supposed educators, how I became recipient of mail promoting materials useful to those in charge of training the young.

The letter at hand is from 'Creative Playthings, Inc.'

Dear Friend: [Creative Playthings says to me, here in a Jerusalem jail] Would you like to foster a creative environment for your students in their own homes? What happens to them after they leave school certainly is important. You may have a child under your direction an average of 25 waking hours per week, but the parents guide him for 45 hours. What a parent does with these hours can complicate or facilitate your program.

We believe the kind of toys Creative Playthings sponsors will genuinely stimulate – in the home – the creative environment you, as an early childhood leader, are trying to foster.

How can Creative Playthings' toys in the home do this?

Such toys can provide for the physical needs of growing children. Such toys help a child discover and experiment with life in the home and community. Such toys promote opportunities for individual expression which may be lacking in the group life of the school.

Such toys help the child work off aggressions. . . .

To which I reply:

Dear Friends: As one who has experimented extensively with life in the home and community, using real people in true-life situations, I doubt that any playthings could prepare a child for one millionth of what is going to hit him in the teeth, ready or not.

My own feeling is that a child should start experimenting with real people and real communities from the moment of birth, if possible. If, for some reason, these materials are not available, then playthings must be used.

But not bland, pleasing, smooth, easily manipulated playthings like those in your brochure, friends! Let there be nothing harmonious about our children's playthings, lest they grow up expecting peace and order, and be eaten alive.

As for children's working off aggressions, I'm against it. They are going to need all the aggressions they can contain for ultimate release in the adult world. Name one great man in history who did not go boiling and bubbling through childhood with a lashed-down safety valve.

Let me tell you that the children in my charge for an average of twenty-five hours a week are not likely to lose their keen edge during the forty-five hours they spend with their parents. They aren't moving hand-carved animals on and off a Noah's Ark, believe me. They are spying on real grownups all the time, learning what they fight about, what they're greedy for, how they satisfy their greed, why and how they lie, what makes them go crazy, the different ways they go crazy, and so on.

I cannot predict the fields in which these children of mine will succeed, but I guarantee success for them without exception, anywhere in the civilized world.

Yours for realistic pedagogy,
Howard W. Campbell, Jr.

The second letter?

It, too, addressed Howard W. Campbell, Jr., as 'Dear Friend,' proving that at least two out of three letter writers today aren't sore at Howard W. Campbell, Jr., at all. The letter is from a stockbroker in Toronto, Canada. It is addressed to the capitalistic aspect of me.

It wants me to buy stock in a tungsten mine in Manitoba. Before I did that, I would have to know more about the company. I would have to know in particular whether it had a capable and reputable management.

I wasn't born yesterday.

The third letter? It is addressed direct to me in prison here.

And – it's a curious letter, indeed. Let it here be seen whole:

Dear Howard:

The discipline of a lifetime now collapses like the fabled walls of Jericho. Who is Joshua, and what is the tune his trumpets play? I wish I knew. The music that has worked such havoc against such old walls is not loud. It is faint, diffuse, and peculiar.

Could it be the music of my conscience: That I doubt. I have done no wrong to you.

I think the music must be an old soldier's itch for just a little treason. And treason this letter is.

I here violate direct and explicit orders that were given to me, were given to me in the best interests of the United States of America. I here give you my true name, and I identify myself as the man you knew as 'Frank Wirtanen.'

My name is Harold J. Sparrow.

My rank at time of retirement from the United States Army was Colonel.

My serial number is 0-61134.

I exist. I can be seen, heard, and touched almost any day, in or around the only dwelling on Coggin's Pond, six miles due west of Hinkleyville, Maine.

I affirm, and will affirm under oath, that I recruited you as an American agent, and that you, at personal sacrifices that proved total, became one of the most effective agents of the Second World War.

If there must be a trial of Howard W. Campbell, Jr., by the forces of self-righteous nationalism, let it be one hell of a contest!

Yours truly,
'Frank'

So I am about to be a free man again, to wander where I please.

I find the prospect nauseating.

I think that tonight is the night I will hang Howard W. Campbell, Jr., for crimes against himself.

I *know* that tonight is the night.

They say that a hanging man hears gorgeous music. Too bad that I, like my father, unlike my musical mother, am tone-deaf. All the same, I hope that the tune I am about to

hear is not Bing Crosby's 'White Christmas.'
Goodbye, cruel world!
Auf wiedersehen?